D1263494

# The Loser

Other translations from Seren

*In Praise of Navigation*
*Twentieth Century Short Stories from the Dutch*

*In a Different Light*
*Fourteen Contemporary Dutch Language Poets*

From the Welsh

*Novels:*

Grahame Davies: *Everything Must Change*
Saunders Lewis: *Monica*
Mihangel Morgan: *Melog*
Kate Roberts: *The Awakening*
Kate Roberts: *Feet in Chains*

*Stories:*

John Gwilym Jones: *The Plum Tree*
Kate Roberts: *Tea in the Heather*

*Poetry:*

Tony Conran: *Welsh Verse*

# The Loser
## Fatos Kongoli

Translated by
Robert Elsie
& Janice Mathie-Heck

**seren**

Seren is the book imprint of
Poetry Wales Press Ltd
57 Nolton Street, Bridgend, CF31 3AE, Wales
www.seren-books.com

© Fatos Kongoli, 2007
translation © Robert Elsie and Janice Mathie-Heck

ISBN 978-1-85411-452-5

First published in Albanian as *I Humburi* by Dituria Publishers, Tirana, in 1992

The right of Fatos Kongoli to be identified as the author of
this work has been asserted in accordance with the Copyright,
Designs and Patents Act, 1988.

A CIP record for this title is available from
the British Library.

This book is a work of fiction. The characters
and incidents portrayed are the work of the author's
imagination. Any other resemblance to actual persons,
living or dead, is entirely coincidental.

All rights reserved. No part of this publication
may be reproduced, stored in a retrieval system,
or transmitted at any time or by any means
electronic, mechanical, photocopying, recording
or otherwise without the prior permission
of the copyright holder.

The publisher works with the financial assistance
of the Welsh Books Council.

Cover photograph: Rhodri Jones

This book has been selected to receive financial assistance from English PEN's
Writers in Translation programme supported by Bloomberg

Printed in Plantin by The Cromwell Press Ltd, Trowbridge

# The Loser

# 1

There comes a day when you get the impression that you've paid your dues to the world, the cycle is complete and there's no more reason to ruminate on the past, in particular when your life has nothing of value to offer. "What now?" you might ask.

Nothing. Just a confession.

One morning a couple of months ago, a friend of mine, Dorian Kamberi, a mechanical engineer and the father of two children, boarded a freighter called the *Partisan* and sailed across the Adriatic with his family. If I hadn't had second thoughts at the last minute, I might be living in some refugee camp in that dreamland called Italy too, or somewhere else in Europe, together with a horde of my countrymen. But at the last minute, as we were sitting on deck squashed like sardines, I told Dori that I was getting off. It's possible that he didn't even hear what I'd said. After the trials and tribulations of our journey – a veritable Odyssey – from town to the ship, my words must have sounded absurd. If anyone other than my friend had been beside me, he'd have chucked me into the sea. Dori said nothing and just gave me a blank stare. The whole time, I could feel the warm pee of his little son, who I was still carrying on my shoulders, trickling down the back of my neck.

My hesitation must have been obvious to everyone. I'm sure that my voice and my face expressed exactly the opposite of what I was saying. Even a small attempt on Dori's part to dissaude me would have been enough to cause me to abandon the decision I'd just taken, not really even knowing why. It wasn't a question of homesickness. I didn't feel anything at all, and my mind was as blank as the expression on Dori's face. He made no move to stop me, and I disembarked, my neck still moist from his son's soggy nappy. I sat down on the edge of the wharf and looked back at the last groups of refugees scrambling to get on board. When the ship set sail and had reached the point where I couldn't see the faces on deck any longer, I felt a lump in my throat. With my head between my hands, I was overcome by a long spell of sobbing. I didn't realize right then that it had been years since I'd last cried. My soul was parched and I'd thought for a long time that nothing more on earth could move me to tears. Someone passing by put his hand on my shoulder and said not to worry, that there would be another freighter docking in the afternoon...

I went back to my neighbourhood at dusk. No one had seen me leave and no one saw me come back. Dorian Kamberi's departure with his family became known the next day. It wasn't the subject of much talk. Some criticized him, some praised him, and others were jealous. I paid attention to the gossip like a thief who has taken part in a robbery and listens to the news of its discovery. For the first time in the forty years of my existence as a bachelor, I had a secret to guard. It was possibly the only secret that my town hadn't found out about. And it would never have found out if I hadn't decided to make this confession. No one would really have been surprised to learn that I'd gone and boarded a freighter to disappear from the face of the earth. But that I should make the tedious journey, get on the ship, and then disembark all of a sudden, no, no one would have believed that. Even Dori, if he'd actually heard what I said, would never have thought that I'd really get off. Maybe he figured that, with my usual sluggishness, I'd have been more of a burden to him than his family, and so he made no attempt to stop me.

Nevertheless, there I was. The next day, my feet carried me out to the cemetery. You might have assumed that it was the grave of some loved one or some sort of nostalgic contemplation which had prevented my departure. This isn't true, though I have a lot of respect for graves and for nostalgia. In fact, I'm envious of people who feel that those kinds of notions are important and provide stability, like the force of gravity, as a basis for action. For myself, I feel I'm somewhere beyond gravity, cast off and abandoned in a black hole of disdain. Nostalgia was a fleeting luxury for me. Those weren't the motives behind my aborted departure or behind my visit the following day – for the first time in my life – to the cemetery. For everyone and from every point of view, I was and am a loser.

★ ★ ★

Grey clouds hovered over the town the next morning. My thoughts were with the refugees at sea. My parents – I live with my mother and father in a two-room apartment plus kitchen – didn't even bother to ask where I'd been the day before. They were used to my absences and had stopped asking me a long time ago where I was going and what I was doing. My coming home at night was enough for them to get a good night's sleep. So my thoughts were with the refugees. I was worried about them because of the bad weather, yet there are certain biological processes inside the human body that take place independent of your emotions. I was starving. I dressed and after a quick and muffled 'morning!' from the doorway, I left my parents to their coffee in the kitchen, and went out.

I don't think there's anywhere on earth quite as dusty as the place I live. There's dust all over, on the flat cement roofs of apartment buildings, on the tiled roofs of private houses, on the pavements and on the flowers poking up in the only park in the centre of town. It sticks to everything, like icing sugar sprinkled on a layer cake in the baker's showcase window. It powders your hair the minute you go outside, deposits itself in your ears and nostrils, gets into your lungs and follows you everywhere you go, to the café, the restaurant, and even into bed. I was about ten years old when they built the cement factory on the riverbank, on the outskirts among the hovels of the gypsy population. It was a construction from past centuries, said those in the know, and produced more dust than it ever did cement. The old people said that it was at exactly that time when the town started to die a slow death.

"You could already be across the ocean," I thought to myself, shuddering as I strolled down the sidewalk. The whole place looked incredibly dingy on that grey March morning, so much so that I almost broke into tears. "You idiot!" I scolded. "What have you done?" I headed straight to the tavern. Normally I'd have gone first to the Riverside Snack Bar to ease my hunger, but there had been rumours circulating recently that its owner, Arsen Mjalti, a one-time foreman at the cement factory, had been using meat of dubious origin for his grilled sausages. There was a lot of gossip about it, ranging from rotten meat taken from dead cows to dog meat, and the gossip was confirmed by plenty of cases of diarrhoea among his customers. They weren't able to come up with proof to give Arsen Mjalti a good beating, and simply boycotted the establishment. So the snack bar was now only patronised by a few good friends of his and by the occasional unwary traveller passing through. It's possible though that the rumours had been spread by a few envious individuals, as some people said that the one-time foreman was making a fortune and that, if he continued, he'd have enough money to buy the famous Hotel Dajti in Tirana.

The tavern was empty. As luck would have it, behind the espresso machine on the counter there was a row of bottles of Scanderbeg cognac which I hadn't indulged in for quite a long time. The waitress at the bar knew exactly what I wanted before I could even open my mouth. She handed me a double cognac to start with, and then made me a coffee. I went over to the window with a glass in one hand and the cup of coffee in the other. Here, customers drank standing up at little elevated tables. Without further delay, I downed the glass of cognac in one quick gulp. I felt terrible and was on the verge of tears. I was hardly able to stifle what would have been a ridiculous scene in front of the waitress. It was only the third double cognac that saved me. Calmer now, and confident that the beast clawing at the depths of my being had been vanquished, I ordered a fourth cognac which I sipped slowly, together with the coffee that I hadn't yet touched. There were few people on the street. Either the heavy clouds of the morning sky had discouraged them from going out, or, as it was a Sunday, they were still sleeping or lying in bed staring at the ceiling, sure that there was nothing of interest to bother going outdoors for. Everyone seemed to be sleeping the sleep of the dead. I wanted to go down to the town square and scream at them: "Wake up, my fellow citizens. Everyone else is gone and you've been left behind!"

I stayed put, sipping away at my cognac until the glass was empty. I ordered a fifth one. I now felt that smooth, velvety sensation under my skin. If you've never tried it, you can't understand what it's like. The world is back on keel and your mind gets sharper. A clarity about what's right and wrong takes over your soul, or it's more like a feeling of righteousness, and you're in a position to make clear decisions without complexes and without worrying. It was then that I decided to take a walk out to the cemetery. I'd never been there before, but at that time it seemed like the most natural thing, something I just had to do and really should have done long ago. I was shocked at the thought that I'd never been. I couldn't know, as I was finishing my fifth glass, that I'd meet a person from town there known as Xhoda the Lunatic. If I had known, I wouldn't have gone.

He was emerging from the graveyard by the gate built into the hole-pocked red brick wall, which was almost as high as a man. For this reason, I didn't see him in time. Otherwise I'd have avoided him. Suddenly there he was in front of me, looking like a vampire looming in a nightmare. He was unshaven, his hair wild in the wind. Xhoda was wearing a military cloak which was open at the front, exposing his hairy chest. For a second, I froze under his piercing stare. He was holding a long iron bar in his hand. He stood as if he might be in deep thought, and gave me an angry glance. As I looked into his bloodshot eyes, I remembered the old saying that even a madman gives way to a drunk. But I was obviously not drunk enough and he wasn't crazy enough. Anyway, I could only get into the graveyard by passing him.

I recovered from my first shock, but I was afraid that he was going to lash out at me. If he had, I could only have ducked and raised my arms to protect myself, just as I'd had to do on several occasions in the past when he was the school headmaster. He'd been on the lookout for a victim among the pupils who he could vent his rage on. I'd been one of his preferred targets. This time he didn't strike me, either with his hand or with the iron bar. He didn't even call me a bastard or a criminal. He just glared with his bloodshot eyes. Unable to meet his glance, I took off.

★ ★ ★

Xhoda the Lunatic was the first person ever to call me 'incorrigible'. I'll always remember the scene in his office when he hurled this accusation at my father who, to show his agreement, gave me a slap in the face to convince me that I really was the person the headmaster accused me of being. If he had gone further, alleging for example that I was a born criminal – although I'd only just turned fourteen at the time – my father would have agreed and slapped me in the face again. My father wasn't really a bad man, but at that moment I hated him more than anyone else, even the headmaster.

I don't remember what the circumstances were when Xhoda first struck me with his cane. It was probably for one of the usual reasons at small-town schools where caning is tacitly accepted, and also because the teachers know perfectly well that the parents won't make a fuss. The beatings took various forms, but all of them involved taking care not to leave any marks on the pupils' bodies. I didn't get beaten until the fifth grade for the simple reason that my teacher for the first four grades didn't believe in corporal punishment for her classes. In the fifth grade we got new teachers whose habits were quite different and, after being passed around from one to the other, we started to realize that we'd been really lucky during our first four years of school. Then it began. I'd never been beaten at home because, as I wanted to say, my father was a placid sort of man. The real head of the family was my mother, but she wasn't in the habit of beating children either. Most of my classmates were the children of ordinary working families, and they got beaten all the time, both at home and at school.

I have a lump in my throat now when I think back to the horror of the moment when I was about to be caned. I had no doubt at all that the time would come. What I didn't realise was that my first punishment would be doled out by the headmaster himself. He was a terrifying man, the only one who even the rowdiest boys would run away from. When he stood before the whole school, the teachers could sense the unease and fear among the mass of pupils and I often had the impression that they were more frightened of him than us kids were. I imagined their fear as being more or less like mine – a fear of the cane in the headmaster's office where I'd never been and where I hoped never to be taken. I was well aware of the fate that was in store for any boy who was sent there.

My first caning was traumatic. I don't remember the reason for it so it had no particular punitive effect. It could have been a complaint from one of the teachers about my being too loud, or a protest from one of the girls whose braids I might have pulled. There might have been other reasons, too... anything. For instance, I might have grinned at the wrong moment or moved from my place in line when the headmaster was making a speech before the school. But it may also just have been my turn because I was one of the few boys in town who hadn't yet felt the headmaster's cane on his back.

After being yanked by the ears and by the hair around my temples and being slapped several times, an experience I was often to go through, I left the headmaster's office without a tear. Dazed, I rushed home to tell my father. I was at the age when children believe that their father is the strongest man on the planet, the person who'll protect them and solve all their problems. This was the origin of my trauma. I hadn't really known my father up to that time and had imagined him as different from what he was. It would take a few more years for me to realise that his wimpy, servile reactions, which cut me to the core, were not merely a result of his normal sluggishness. The next day, he came with me to the headmaster's office. If I'd suspected that he was going to degrade himself to *that* extent, I'd never have told him about the beating. I'd have preferred being beaten ten times a day rather than see the terror in my father's eyes. Humiliating scenes like that would repeat themselves often, with the only difference that my father, who had never struck me, would later become accustomed to doing it and would carry out this activity with passion every time he was summoned to school by Xhoda the Lunatic to learn of my mischievous deeds. This went on until I reached the seventh grade when Xhoda pronounced the fatal word 'incorrigible' and I really got caned. From that time on, I think I became incorrigible for good.

But let me return to that day when, after the first beating, I made the fatal discovery: my father wasn't strong at all. He was a coward just like the rest of them, like the teachers and everyone else who quivered in Xhoda's shadow. I was twelve years old then, and still in the fifth grade. Now, almost thirty years later, I can state with conviction that I wept more tears that afternoon than I would for the rest of my life. And I ran away from home. They found me in Tirana the next day asleep on a bench in the park across from the Hotel Dajti. I was in a state of exhaustion, starving and frightened. I didn't know that this naïve disappointment would become the first of a whole series of disappointments. Yet I experienced none of them with such tragic intensity as this one because my father was now dead to me, and the damage done couldn't be repaired. Xhoda had destroyed the vision I'd cherished of my father, and so I decided, in my way, to take revenge.

★ ★ ★

We were living at the time in the same apartment – two rooms and a kitchen – where we live now. I had, and have, one sister who is five years older than me, but she plays no role in my story, if I can call the mediocrity of my earthly existence a story. The chronicle of my life is certainly mediocre. It's the story of a man who never was and never turned out to be anything, an anonymous existence melded into the anonymity of an obscure neighbourhood in an obscure town, even though it's not far from the capital city. My sister spent most of her time away from home. When I was little, she was at the teacher-training boarding school, and later, when she got a job, she was appointed as a teacher in a village in the north of the country, where she's been ever since.

My apartment building is near the centre of town. Across the road, on the other side of the park and the paved square, there's another apartment building. On the ground floor there are various food stores, a fabric shop, a tailor and a café. The café has made the apartment building and the whole square well known in town. The most spectacular brawls between individuals and rival groups have happened here. The town didn't take them particularly seriously, probably because the residents considered brawls like that to be a normal part of everyday life, just as it later became normal to sit around and watch films on TV. There was no television in town at that time, and yet there was no shortage of news. Most of the residents were of the impression that dust played a decisive role in all newsworthy happenings. In conjunction with the vapours of alcohol, it drove my fellow citizens to foolishness. They're a passionate bunch and excessively jealous – two things which don't belong in an atmosphere of peace and quiet. As well as this, most of them are workers with strong arms and quick fists. What else could be needed to make headlines? But the town news was never written down. Interested sociologists are advised to contact the local authorities, who, I hope, might still have records of those kinds of events. Maybe they even have a file on a certain Thesar Lumi. That's me.

I say 'maybe' because it seems to me that I'm making a bit too much of myself, thinking that there might be a whole file on me. I was and still am thoroughly insignificant and, in thinking about the possible existence of a file on me, I certainly don't dare to compare myself to people who are worthy of an honour like that. Yet I do take pride in believing those who insist that you don't have to be important to have a file. All you have to do is cast a shadow on this earth. I'd be more than happy if this were the case, because it would mean that, at a time when I considered myself non-existent in this world, there were others who had a different opinion. And I'm grateful to them.

To give myself a pat on the back, I'll assume that there was a file on me. I don't know what could possibly have been written in it and most likely I'll never find out, but one thing I can say for sure: the real facts, which might in one way or another be construed as criminal activities, are missing. They can't be in the file because, when I committed them, I was still a boy. I committed them at the time when, for no comprehensible reason, my father suddenly submitted to the will of Xhoda the Lunatic and I lost all my respect for him. So I decided to take revenge.

## The Loser >>

At this point in my story, I should mention Vilma, or what is really my memory of her. Vilma no longer exists. She's been gone for a long time.

# 2

My brain tends to confuse periods of time so that I'm not sure whether Vilma was already every boy's dream when I was little. I don't know whether she'd already been destined at that age to play the role of an apple of discord in a town of rowdies. My sluggish mind has trouble piercing the layers of past years – that curtain of fog behind which the universe of my childhood and my vision of Vilma lie. I was just a child when I got to know her, although I thought of myself as a man. Boys grow up quickly in a small town like that.

I can see her beyond that curtain of fog. There she is, standing behind the wrought-iron fence. She always used to stand there, watching passers-by out on the street. Today passers-by can see Xhoda the Lunatic sitting on a bench behind that same black fence, with the wild eyes of a madman. He stations himself there like a guard dog. His insanity consists of the fact that he believes his daughter is still behind the fence, and he's poised to attack any potential foes with that iron bar in his hand. Poor devil. He didn't realize that Vilma was untouchable. He didn't know that his menacing shadow wouldn't have been able to defend her against anyone. There was something else that protected Vilma, and woe to any guy who dared to touch even a strand of her hair. Even if he'd deployed a hundred guard dogs around the house or had sent a hundred hounds out to follow her in the streets, they wouldn't have protected his daughter as well as Fagu.

It's exasperating. It drives me crazy. I want to talk about Vilma, yet it's the spectre of Fagu which rises in front of me. I want to recall her shining eyes which were the colour of the deep blue sea, but in front of me I see his black eyes, always full of anger. It's hard, but I manage to grope my

way through the thick fog in search of that placid, intelligent face, and I only come across Fagu's eternally gloomy
glare. The two faces will be linked to one another for the
rest of my days. Every time I imagine one, the other
appears and drives it away. And then, there's the terrible
moment when I see the two faces superimposed on each
other. A Vilmafagu or a Faguvilma. Everything becomes
distorted and vague. They are mutilated and have no
expression. Death and decomposition couldn't do more to
disfigure a face. Sometimes, though not very often, this
vision tortures me in my sleep and makes me painfully
aware that I'll never be able to get rid of it. Soaked in sweat,
I wake up, my heart almost bursting in my chest. Then,
transfixed under the spell of the nightmare, I spend all day
at the tavern. Things only get moving after the first double
cognac which seems to act as a lubricant, making its way
through my blood vessels to my brain and greasing the
rusty shell of my sub-cortex. Then things start to happen.
More glasses follow and precipitate my lethargic liberation.
But it's still too early. The movement stops there. Most of
Vilma's mouth and her closed lips are stuck between
Fagu's teeth. Her nose shifts a bit, her eyes, too, and then
the contours of her face. From experience I know that after
the first glass, half of Vilma's face is still covered by half of
Fagu's, while the other halves are free. I have to be quick
with the next glass because I can't bear this part of the
vision. Once the third double is down the hatch, the two
faces hardly touch each other and, by the fourth, they're
completely separated. I need a fifth for Fagu's awful scowl
to disappear and, finally, to be alone with Vilma.

There she is, behind the bars of the wrought-iron fence.
She's wearing that white dress, a belt around her waist, and
with waves of her long hair flowing down over her shoulders. She's blonde, so in the sun her hair shines like the
Golden Fleece. I'm fairly sure that her dress is made of the
same material as bridal gowns. The plan I cooked up to
take revenge on Xhoda wasn't to kidnap her and make her

my bride, although dressed like that, she looked a lot like one. I stared at her with the eyes of a common thug, someone with criminal intent on his mind. What my exact intent was, I'll reveal later. First of all, though, I have to make clear something which all the guys of my generation in town knew, that whole pack of twelve and thirteen-year-old rascals: Vilma belonged to Fagu. So she was closely watched over by his gang, whose members were among the toughest kids at school. Vilma was aware of this, too. She was twelve, like me. Fagu was thirteen, a whole year older.

I can't say what opinion Vilma had of the status she'd been given by the others. I never really thought much about it. There was a convention which I accepted, as everyone of my age did, playfully learning the mummy-daddy game, that every boy should have a girl. As for me, I was reserved and didn't take a role. Actually, I thought they were all crazy and that it was undignified for a boy to spend his time hanging around girls. If Fagu wanted to keep playing that ridiculous mummy-daddy charade with Vilma, it was his business. I saw him as trapped and was surprised that all that gang of thugs at school would accept Fagu as their leader. To put it briefly, Vilma wouldn't have entered my life to that extent and in that way, if I hadn't seized on the idea of taking revenge on Xhoda.

I often tried to convince myself that it was all a game of coincidence, of luck, but like everyone else in my generation, I was raised with not even a speck of religious education. I've heard it said that religious people take comfort and find peace of mind in expressions such as 'thus it was written'. A religious person believes in a predetermined fate. But how was I, who believed in nothing, to find consolation? I don't think that the wicked will expiate their evil deeds in the flames of hell, and I don't believe that those who are good will be compensated in heaven. But I would like to believe that there's something like a last judgment. I hang on to this faint hope because it's the only thing that keeps me going in the endless futility of my existence.

I soon realised that taking revenge on Xhoda wouldn't be easy. At first, I considered smashing the windows of his house, a detached building away from the centre of town and surrounded by a high wrought-iron fence covered with plants and creeping vines. There was an alley nearby and it would be the place where I could shatter all the glass in the windows. But I gave up on the idea. During the day, it was impossible to act without being noticed due to all the passers-by, and I was afraid to go out at night because the town was infested with packs of wild dogs. I also gave up the scheme of hiding a snake in the drawer of the head-master's desk, not because it was impossible to find a snake – the gypsies who lived down by the river would have caught one for me anytime – but, firstly it was virtually impossible to get into his office, and secondly it was even more impossible to pry open the drawer of his desk. Three similar attempts had been made at school and all of them had failed. So I'd have to come up with some other method of taking revenge. And I did.

I stumbled on the idea by sheer coincidence. One day, in the schoolyard where Fagu's gang was hanging around, I came across a scene which was nothing unusual in itself. Fagu was beating up a boy who lived down by the river, while the members of his gang were looking on. All the other boys were watching from a distance and everything was happening in silence. The gypsy boy put up with the beating without saying a word until Fagu had had his fill and let him go, giving him a final kick in the ass. It was unthinkable that anyone would help a gypsy. He was a short, chunky, apathetic kid, one of the few children from the riverside who attended school regularly. His name was Sherif and he was in the fifth grade, in class A, whereas I was in class C. I knew something else about him that was important. His father, a stubby gypsy, as apathetic as his son, was given the task at various times of the year of exter-minating the wild dogs. It was said that if he didn't do it, the dogs would overrun and destroy the whole town. To get this done, he relied on pieces of poisoned beef liver, which had an immediate effect.

The bell rang and recess was over. The schoolyard behind the building emptied. Sherif stayed by himself in a corner. I'm not sure what prompted me to go over and speak to him. Either I felt sorry for him or I just despised Fagu. And I definitely did despise Fagu. He was a brutal braggart. In any case, I learned something I wouldn't forget. Fagu had beaten up Sherif because Sherif had teased Vilma in class the day before, and she had complained to Fagu. What a beast she was, just like her father! In fact, all three of them were beasts: her henchman father, Vilma and that street tough who debased himself even more by giving into her whims. It didn't take much convincing to make Sherif my accomplice.

★ ★ ★

I played the game with exemplary hypocrisy. I stress the word hypocrisy. At the time, I didn't know what the word meant, but around that age, hypocrisy got under my skin and into my blood. If someone had explained it to me, maybe I wouldn't have become the way I was. But no-one explained it to me. From the first grade at school we'd had lessons in moral education, yet I don't remember any teacher ever explaining the meaning of hypocrisy to us. I do recall something else – that the teachers acted differently in the principal's presence than they did when he wasn't around. They often lied blatantly to him while we were there, but none of us said a word. We hated Xhoda as much as we were scared of him. We felt the same way about the teachers. I'd noticed that whenever a school inspector turned up, the headmaster would act peculiar. He was kinder and more polite, and lied to the inspector, in the very same way the teachers lied to him. And things turned out alright for him. We were raised to believe that we were the happiest children on earth. That was what the songs we learned taught us.

Nevertheless, I had reason to doubt whether we were really the happiest children on earth. I can't speak for the others, but at home, I often saw scenes between my parents which were so violent that they sent shivers down my spine. To prevent any misunderstanding, I should say that my father had no particular vices. He didn't indulge in alcohol or tobacco and I'm convinced that he wasn't much of a lady's man. It was my mother who wore the pants in our family. Father was head of the bookkeeping division at work and mother was a seamstress. I knew they tried not to fight when I was there, but they didn't always succeed. What surprised me on most occasions was that the disputes were set off by completely insignificant things. I'd never have fought with my friends over that kind of absurd stuff. Anyway, the storm clouds would gather, bringing insults, accusations and counter-accusations. The first to get tired of the disputes was my father. Deprived of a worthy opponent, my mother would sniff defiantly and calm down, too. Then, when the room was full of a deafening silence, I would hear my father lament: "God, what a dog's life!" So I concluded that nobody could live as the happiest child on earth, as we were told in the songs we learned, and, at the same time, live a dog's life, as my father maintained. My conclusion totally confused me and brought me face to face with another curious phenomenon – the theatrical talents of my parents. It's hard for me to speak about this, but it's true. My parents were consummate actors.

There was a certain fellow named Hulusi who lived in our apartment building. He's dead now. He was a short guy and used to come over quite often. I remember that he could consume an enormous amount, and it often happened that he wouldn't budge until he'd downed a whole bottle of raki. From the way my parents talked about him, I had the impression that, at the first possible chance, they'd grab him and throw him out the window. Anyway, that's what I heard my father say. But the scene which I'd been waiting to witness for a long time, and that I believed would take place, that is, my father chucking Hulusi, half his size, out the window, never happened. I could hardly wait for my father to grab Hulusi by the neck the second he came into the room, and yet my father and mother beamed hospitably at him. Hulusi helped himself to the raki and stayed as long as he wanted. As soon as he was gone, the smiling masks on my parents' faces disappeared. Father stuck his fists into his pockets and started to pace up and down the room like a tiger. Mother fell silent. Hulusi, so despised and looked down on as he was, turned out to be our family's guardian angel. Without his assistance, my sister would never have been able to attend the teacher training college and, later, I'd never have had a chance to go to university. But I didn't know that at the time. I wasn't aware that our neighbour, Hulusi, who lived one floor above us, was the real power behind the throne in our town. And I wasn't aware that to gain the good graces of our guardian angel, my parents had to pay eternal tribute – the loss of their dignity. There were lots of other things I didn't know, things which life would later teach me, one by one. In those years, my brain offered me a very simple and easy, in fact I'd say conformist, explanation for all these big dilemmas – everyone around me was an actor, including my teachers and my parents. They would put on and take off their masks whenever it suited them. In the same way, I'd have to find masks of my own, just as the grown-ups had. This was the definitive solution to the quandary. Concerning the dilemma as to whether we were the happiest children on earth, I'd come up with an explanation which you might even call original. We were and were not. It was like the mangy dogs roaming around town. I couldn't imagine these animals being happy. They got kicked around wherever they went, not to mention the poisoned liver which Sherif's father put out for them. Pet dogs, on the other hand (most families with houses and gardens kept a dog), in particular lap dogs, I considered to be the happiest species on earth. Even Vilma had a lap dog. It was white and had curly hair.

Vilma was the apple of Xhoda's eye. The lap dog was the apple of Vilma's eye. I decided to poison Vilma's dog.

# 3

I poisoned Vilma's white lap dog to take revenge. There wasn't any other reason for doing it. As a child, I considered myself equal to all the other kids in the sense of social equality, or rather, to the extent a twelve-year-old can understand the concept of social equality. I'm sure that I had no complexes and didn't see myself as descending from a race of mongrels – as belonging to a species of wretches – and I didn't see Vilma as stemming from a race of lap dogs – a species of the chosen few. It was only later that I'd learn that Vilma and I belonged to different species. This was to be my second trauma. But at the time, I was still under the influence of the first trauma when, after the beating, I lost all respect for my father. Vilma's puppy would have to pay, even if it meant that Vilma would be in tears for days and nights on end and that Xhoda would rage and lose his mind.

It was a beautiful lap dog, and like all others of its kind it would rush out and bark wildly, sticking its nose through the pickets of the fence whenever anyone walked by. It barked at me that way, too. It was a warm afternoon and Vilma was sitting in her little chair near the stairs, concentrating on her book. She didn't look up when the barking started. But since I didn't budge, it started lunging at me furiously, yelping loud enough to wake up the whole neighbourhood. I'd counted on this. Annoyed, Vilma finally raised her head. Her eyes caught mine... and mine caught hers. They were azure blue like the ocean. We recognised one another, but we'd never spoken because we'd always been in different classes at school. And, to tell the truth, I really had no desire to speak to Vilma right then.

First she frowned and then shouted something like "Max, be quiet, get back here!" As Max had no intention of obeying, she got up, tossed her book on the chair, and ran towards us. I stood there bewildered. Max only calmed down when his mistress picked him up. I blushed and attempted a smile. I told her she had a beautiful dog. "Don't say that," replied Vilma. "He'll get all stuck-up if he hears you and he'll start biting everyone who walks past the house."

All of a sudden I turned and bolted. Vilma stood there at the fence with Max. Years later, she reminded me of the scene. "You were so strange, the way you stared at me, looking right into my eyes! I went back to the stairs with Max and pretended I was reading, but actually I was waiting for you to come back and stare into my eyes again. No boy had ever looked at me that way and I didn't understand what it was that made me wait for you. I never stopped believing that you'd re-appear at the fence one day, even later when you were going to university and rumours had spread in town that you were having an affair with a widow. But you never turned up. I waited for you, even though you poisoned my Max. I cried for him as I would have for a brother. And yet, I waited for you, though I was convinced you'd never come back."

From the moment I started to run, I was convinced, too, that I wouldn't go back. When Vilma picked Max up and started to talk to me, I knew that if I stayed any longer, I wouldn't be able to take revenge at all. I don't know how to explain it properly, but I felt that if I hung around near Vilma, listening to her voice, looking into her eyes and watching her pet the dog, I wouldn't feel up to poisoning Max. And if I didn't poison Max, Vilma wouldn't cry. And if Vilma didn't cry, Xhoda wouldn't lose his mind.

Max had a painful but quick end. Before we committed the crime, Sherif asked me to find out what food the dog preferred. With some trouble, I found out from a boy who used to visit Vilma quite often – they were cousins – that Max loved fried liver, preferably lamb. I got some. Without his father noticing, Sherif mixed it with the poison used to

exterminate wild dogs. We did away with Max one afternoon while Vilma was taking him out for a walk, as she
often did, to the edge of town where the fields start. Sherif
reported to me that it was no problem getting the dog to
eat the bait while Vilma was busy talking to a girlfriend.
Max gave up the ghost almost instantly. Right after, everything spun out of control.

Sherif came over the next evening. He'd never been to
my house and when I saw him leaning against the banister
in the stairwell, I suspected something had happened.
Another thing worried me, too. Sherif hadn't turned up for
school that day. He looked scared and asked me to come
out so that we could talk somewhere in private where we
wouldn't be seen or heard. It was dark, so we managed to
get through the centre of town without being seen and
reached the neighbourhood near the riverbank. We
crouched there in the bushes. Sherif was shaking and
started to cry. Then I understood what had happened. A
state of emergency had been declared in town the moment
word of Max's demise spread. "After lunch," Sherif
explained, "the headmaster came over with two policemen.
I don't know what they talked about outside, but my dad
came back into the house furious and clenched his fist at
me. He made a threat: 'I'll kill you with my own bare hands
if I ever find out that you were involved in this business.'"

Poor Sherif was frightened to death. He was sure that
his father was going to kill him. But this was nothing
compared to another even more terrifying aspect. Even
though Sherif hadn't gone to school that day, Fagu and his
gang were able to find him down by the river. Everyone
suspected Sherif. They beat him up and said they'd murder
him if he didn't tell them the truth. Sherif denied everything. It was the fact that he'd denied the whole affair that
made his position so precarious. No one believed him,
including his father and Fagu. Now, with tears in his eyes,
he kissed my hand (I'll never forget how he bent over to
kiss it) and begged me to save him. Otherwise he'd have no

choice but to throw himself into the river and drown.

I didn't need time to think about it. Sherif was petrified. I'd got him involved in the affair, so I was obligated to do something. I had to assume responsibility, and that's what I did. Not because I was afraid that he would actually kill himself, although, given the circumstances, I believed he could have. I decided to admit to being the perpetrator of the crime because I felt that I could stand the torments of hell better than his slobbery kisses on my hand. If I didn't own up, Sherif would come around every day and lick my hand like a beaten dog.

I confessed to Fagu. This way, I was sure the news would be spread instantly in the right direction and yet I'd have enough time to prepare myself for the inevitable. Fagu glared at me. It was the most incredible thing he'd ever heard. He only believed me when I explained to him that I'd committed the murder to take revenge on Xhoda. Everyone knew that Xhoda had beaten me up recently. So vengeance would be seen as justified, even in this form. Fagu couldn't touch me personally. If he did, he'd be in trouble himself. None of the tough guys in his gang would have forgiven him for beating me up just for Vilma's sake.

Events took their course. Fagu, at that time, was bigger than I was, and, most definitely stronger, too. He foamed at the mouth, but just sneered at me and left. From that day on, my life became unbearable. Everyone stared at me as if I were a criminal. At school, when we were lined up in the courtyard, what I'd done was denounced as the most dastardly event ever to have taken place in that town. My grade for behaviour was reduced by two marks and I was suspended from school for three days. My first caning didn't come from Xhoda, who didn't even deign to call me into his office, but from my father. I wasn't expecting it because he'd never beaten me before. The beating happened when he got back from the police station where he'd been summoned to account for my behaviour. I also discovered that he'd paid compensation to Xhoda, an amount of around three or four thousand leks. To this very day, I don't know if my father beat me because of the crime itself, because of the money he was forced to pay or because of the dread he felt all through his body when he was called to the police station. Whatever the reason, from that time on, my father acquired a taste for caning me. He learned how to beat me, but I also learned how to take a beating. Once you get used to it, nothing else makes much of an impression.

"You stupid idiot," I thought to myself as I turned my back on Xhoda and left him standing at the cemetery gate with an iron bar in his hand. We were meant to while away the days together. It seemed as if we were made to torture each other. As I walked down the dusty path, I wondered whether I'd been destined by fate to be a curse on Xhoda in the days of his insanity, or if his insanity might be a fore-warning that I'd never find tranquillity.

My tears started to fall, proving that the gleam in Xhoda's bloodshot eyes had sobered me up. The grey sky hanging overhead like a dirty sheet, reminded me of the refugees out at sea. Suddenly I could smell urine. Was it the smell of the pee of Dori's little boy? Maybe it was the smell of my tears. I was crying, and that meant that the alcohol had worn off. Maybe I was weeping for the refugees out at sea. I went back to the tavern, but they were unfortunately out of cognac. I had no choice but to head for the Riverside Snack Bar, but it wasn't open. Apparently, the one-time foreman of the cement factory, Arsen Mjalti, had put on weight and, like a few of his colleagues, was allowing himself the luxury of a day off on Sundays.

The town still looked dead, in spite of the amount of cognac I'd imbibed. I was on the verge of returning to the centre and shouting: "Wake up, citizens of the town. From this day on you are free men and may go wherever you desire. Your long-awaited freedom has dawned and you may leave by land, sea or air. No one will call you traitors, no one will call you hooligans. Social justice has triumphed."

I decided not to shout, and I didn't go back to the town centre. I no longer felt like crying, a sign that I was drunk once again without having swilled any more cognac. Then

I noticed Xhoda the Lunatic wandering through the streets and I followed him back to his house. His silhouette disappeared in the doorway. For a second, I don't know what came over me, but I had the impression that a white yelping ball of fur had leapt out of the dark entrance. It took my breath away and I covered my face to protect myself. It couldn't be Max. I'd killed him thirty years ago. I leaned my head against the trunk of a pine tree nearby and felt queasy. I felt like I was being stuffed with a hunk of poisoned liver, and threw up. When I looked up through my wet eyelashes, I caught a glimpse of Xhoda the Lunatic in the distance, sitting in his armchair at the head of the stairs with an iron bar in his hand. "Get out of here, you poor fool!" I wanted to yell out. "Oh, sphinx of tragedy, what secret are you harbouring?"

# 4

That pine tree had been thirty years younger and I was so thin that I could hide behind it. Vilma was sitting in her chair reading a book. I'd been watching her for over an hour and she hadn't raised her head even once. There was no Max to rush out and bark by the fence. He was dead. I stood there cringing behind the trunk of the pine tree. I was sure that Vilma knew I was there. I was lost in thought when suddenly I felt something at my feet. I picked it up. It was a stone wrapped in paper. "Are you sorry for what you did? Is that what you've come to tell me? Don't even bother. You've been hiding behind that tree for five days now, like a robber. Even if you say you're sorry, I won't forgive you. Why Max? What did Max ever do to you? Even if you have an answer, I know that I'll always hate you."

When I looked up, the chair where Vilma had been sitting was empty. This is the last vision of my childhood that I can recall. Everything else is gone. All that's left is the empty chair, as if to remind me of the emptiness of my existence. I felt no regret for my crime. Even when I read Vilma's note, I didn't understand why she'd reacted the way she had. My wish to glimpse her golden hair in secret from behind the pine tree had nothing to do with regret. But now that Vilma had rejected me, there was nothing more for me to do but leave. And never return. I suffered because I couldn't stare at her hair anymore from behind the pine tree, and with this suffering my inferiority complex grew. It was then that I put my childhood behind me – with the discovery that there was a feeling that people called inferiority.

It was on one of those evenings that Hulusi, a top official in our little town, ranting and full of raki, stumbled his way up the staircase to the floor above us, and fell into bed.

In our apartment he left behind not only the stench of alcohol and a mess on the kitchen table, but my poor parents who were at the end of their rope. From today's perspective, I'd call the whole affair a tragicomedy. Sometimes I even enjoyed seeing the strain on their faces. But that night went too far. I believe it was the first and last time that my father, for reasons only he understood, ever attempted to keep up with Hulusi, glass after glass. I remember seeing my mother enter and leave the kitchen in a fit as the men got drunker and drunker. As opposed to Hulusi who babbled incessantly, my father listened without saying a word. He might not have even been listening. When Hulusi finally left and my mother closed the door behind him, my father made an obscene gesture, the meaning of which was perfectly clear to me as a young man. There's no need to explain it. Then he got the hiccups and staggered back into the kitchen, where he made a speech, the essence of which was: "If your brother wasn't such a son of a bitch, this other son of a bitch wouldn't be making my life so miserable. But since your brother's the real son of a bitch he is, he's left me in this bind and I don't know how to get out of it. Do you know what I mean by a bind?"

My mother let out a scream. This was enough to sober my father up right away. After the scream, she rushed out of the kitchen and locked herself in the bedroom. Father stood there like a tree trunk struck by lightning. I was sitting on the sofa in the corner, and I didn't know what to do. Both mother and father had forgotten I was in the room. But maybe they were too upset and my being there was simply not enough to bring them to their senses. Father covered his mouth with his hands. He went over to the table and slumped onto a chair and then I saw him break into tears. My mouth was parched. His heavy body was bent over. He was shaking and the whole table, even the walls, seemed to shake along with him. I sat there, caught between my desire to run away and my fear that father might look up and see me. Fighting back my tears, I finally tiptoed out of the kitchen and locked myself in my room. There, where no one could see me, I dissolved into sobs. I hadn't understood a word of my father's speech and my mother had only let out a scream, but I realised something had happened that evening that was more ominous than the many other arguments I'd seen my parents have. Later, I decided not to delve into the deeper meaning of my father's words, or of my mother's scream. I felt it wasn't right to stick my nose into things that only involved their lives. While I was leaning against the door of my bedroom, really upset at my father's sobbing, I also remember hearing his voice in the corridor. I listened closely. He was begging mother to forgive him. In a whisper he swore he'd never repeat what he'd said, that it was the first and last time he'd ever get drunk. Mother kept silent and he begged her again and again. I don't know what I felt more for him at that moment: pity or disgust. Mother refused to open the door so he spent the night in the kitchen. When I heard him snoring, I was convinced that mother would be asleep now, too.

I think I got to sleep myself just before dawn. When I woke up, the sunlight was already flooding into my bedroom. Then I understood that I didn't have to go to school that day. My parents had let me sleep in. I was still disturbed by what had happened. I was surprised when my parents didn't go to work. They were sitting at the kitchen table, across from each other, drinking coffee. Something infuriated me when I saw them calmly sipping their drinks as if nothing had happened the night before. I felt like a tiger in a cage and the more affection they showed me, the angrier I became. I wanted to shout, break something, sneer and spit at them, use the filthiest words I knew to insult them, stick out my tongue – in short, utilize my whole arsenal of forbidden gestures and acts that I'd been taught not to use. They pretended not to notice anything, though maybe I gave them no reason to be suspicious. I only asked one question. I wanted to know who this brother of my mother was. Up to that moment, I'd had no idea that my mother had a brother, and that I had an uncle.

Mother dropped her cup and father turned white. And that's how I was destined at that young age to learn that I belonged to a category of inferior beings or, as I imagined it at the time, to a category of mangy mongrels who are kicked around wherever they go. As pale as death itself, my father revealed to me in brief terms that I did in fact have an uncle. "Several months after you were born," he explained, "your uncle, who was doing his military service, crossed over the border with two companions. He fled the country, was declared an enemy of the people and became a shame on our family. He no longer exists for any of us, not for you either. You need to hate him."

This is how father ended his brief explanation, telling me that I was to hate someone who, up to that moment, I hadn't known existed. In fact, there was no need for father to insist on it – that I should hate that person, even though he was my mother's brother and therefore my own uncle. We had already learned at that tender age that anyone who fled the country was a monster. I knew a boy in town whose brother had fled the country. His name was Rik. The other boys avoided him and no one wanted to play with him. It was as if he had a contagious disease that everyone was afraid of catching. I avoided him, too. Rik's solitary house, an earthen hovel with a tiled roof at the edge of town, was located out in the fields, far from the main road. It was a mysterious cottage, frightening in our imagination, and because no one visited it, we thought it was haunted. That was why my father didn't need to insist on my hating an unknown individual. The fact that the uncle in question had fled the country was quite sufficient.

It's not likely that my parents understood the effect this discovery had on me. In actual fact, my thoughts at that moment were with Vilma. My parents would never have imagined that there was a connection between the shock of my expression and Vilma. I was thinking that I'd now no longer be able to go to her house and hide behind the pine tree to catch a glimpse of her hair. I had an uncle who'd fled the country and, because of that, or so I thought, I wasn't worthy of winning Vilma's affection. But my parents wouldn't have understood this. Father, looking me straight in the eyes, impressed on me one important thing. Under no circumstance, at any moment, was I ever to mention my uncle – to anyone. While he was staring at me, Rik's house appeared in my mind, shrouded in solitude and sorrow. I could see Rik himself, always scared and elusive like a shadow. If, in religious terms, my parents had ever committed any sin against me, it was on that day. And a two-fold sin at that. They demanded that I should hate someone I didn't know, even though he was my uncle, and they demanded that I should hate him silently, surreptitiously. So, in religious terms, I was led down the path of unrighteousness. A few days earlier I had killed Max. This crime committed by a child didn't bother my conscience. I'd shown the courage to admit to it with all its consequences. Under those circumstances, Max's death couldn't really be called a sin and, because I'd committed no other sin up to that day, it didn't count as my first. I see myself as first having sinned from the moment my father told me to hate someone I didn't know. There was no way I could hate a figment of my imagination, either openly or secretly. The emotional deformation – my path to eternal damnation – started when I accepted to bear inside me a burning, frightening and dangerous secret. I was aware that my parents also harboured this secret. In an attempt at damage-control, they had moved to our town shortly after the escape of my infamous uncle, the one who had stained our reputation forever. To a certain extent, they succeeded.

From that day on, the world had only two colours for me: black and white. It consisted of two communities: the whites (Vilma) and the blacks (me). From that day on, I lived with the illusion that I was residing in the universe of the whites, knowing full well that I belonged to the community of the blacks. I started to accustom myself to the dichotomy, and to an eternal guilt complex. And the dream that started to crystallise inside me to overcome the impasse was my desire to escape. Not in the sense of physical escape. I'd tried that and knew what it was like. I escaped within myself, off to horizons of solitude. There's no more depressing escape than this, but at least it's safe. From then on, I concentrated my life on the dusty banalities of our little town, a soporific monotony interrupted either by a caning from Xhoda at school or a caning from my father at home, or from both. But eventually the beatings came to an end. I can't remember the exact date. Though I can recall my first beating by Xhoda and by my father, I simply can't remember the last occasion from either one of them. It's quite understandable. The last caning was merely part of the daily routine and exited from my memory without leaving a trace. One thing I can say for certain. It was at the time when Vilma had almost completely disappeared from my life, just like Fagu, Xhoda, my parents and the whole little town. The entire period has been wiped out of my memory, like the last beating. For obvious reasons, I didn't attend high school in that town. This reduced the danger of the biographical time bomb of our family's past being discovered, which would have destroyed my whole future. I was intent, following the example of my sister, on getting as far away as I could from the town and the people who knew me there and who might regard me as competition. Hulusi, our eternal benefactor and guardian angel, that mysterious person, with even more mysterious links to my parents, came to my assistance and disappeared from my life without ever really having entered it. With his help, I was able to register at a high school in Tirana. He also helped to get me into university, to read industrial chemistry. Hulusi died unexpectedly three months after I began my studies. I didn't attend his funeral, but I prayed that his soul would go to heaven. I hope it did. Meanwhile, Ladi had come into my life.

# 5

I'd like to pause here and catch my breath. I want to fill my lungs with air and soar into the realm of oblivion. Impossible. I can't go on without talking about Ladi, because the pain I feel on account of him is just as strong as the pain I felt for Vilma.

His name was Vladimir, but like everyone else, I called him Ladi. He was part of the generation when that name was very popular and you could find dozens of Vladimirs in every school and neighbourhood, even though they weren't actually born on the day of the Orthodox Saint Vladimir. So he had an Orthodox name and, although he wasn't of that faith, he was of a strict orthodox persuasion of a different kind. Ladi was tall and thin, and a quiet boy. He wore jeans, which were rare then (I'm speaking about the early seventies). In the wintertime, he used to wrap a long scarf around his neck because he often had problems with his tonsils, and in spite of his frequent suffering, I was surprised that they were never operated on, either when he was a boy or later.

I noticed something from our very first lectures. The professors treated him with unusual respect. This was particularly true of the head of the chair, a short and energetic individual with thinning hair who I called Xhohu – from the first syllables of Xhoda and Hulusi. This was because Xhohu had both the physical appearance of Xhoda and the manners of Hulusi. So, from now on, I won't call him by his real name, but Xhohu, since I don't want to underestimate his intellectual capacities, although I should add that the presence of Ladi was enough to make him forget who he was and to turn him into a fawning sycophant. Ladi's father was a high official in the Party hierarchy. This explains another phenomenon. Ladi was rarely by himself. He was always with other young guys and girls. As far as I was concerned, I had enough reasons not to approach him, not to mention the fact that I'd been a bit of an introvert for quite a while. I avoided people and opportunities to make friends, and tried to remain as inconspicuous as possible. I'd worked at this for years during high school and so I entered university with the self-confidence of a master whose art was composure and self-control. It was painful to have to wear a mask like that at an age when the wish to make a good appearance and to show off is greater than at any other time. Nevertheless, the strategy I'd chosen gave me the advantage of being able to observe others and watch how they behaved, and I must admit that I often found this quite enjoyable. Nothing could compare to the enjoyment of observing Xhohu's behaviour. I was really convinced of this when I became friends with Ladi, but I'll return to that later. For now, I'd just like to mention that, as opposed to others who fawned over Ladi and were convinced that he was happy – after all, he had everything that anyone would ever want – I had the impression that, like me but in a different way, he was wearing a mask just like an actor's in an attempt to cover up something specific: the sadness in his eyes. In this respect, he wasn't a good actor, no mistake about that. Nevertheless, for obvious reasons, I didn't try to approach him. Ladi was surrounded by his colourful panoply of companions, male and female, and he had no reason to notice me among the eighty students of the first year. But I was wrong.

By sheer coincidence, one rainy November afternoon, I happened to sit down with him at a table in the back room of a café in the Palace of Culture. Nowadays, it's a rundown joint and, aside from the obviously bored waitresses and empty counter, you can only find a few young people smoking with a cup of fake coffee in front of them or, at best, a glass of that disgusting Iliria cognac. But at that time, it was quite a posh place and the service was excellent by the standards of the capital. It attracted somewhat of a snobbish elite many of whom were the sons and daughters of government officials. I hadn't been there before because I'd never had the money, but I went into the 'Palace' that day because it was raining outside, just for fun to see what was going on. Ladi was sitting at a table in the middle of the room and, when he waved, I wasn't sure at first that he was waving at me. He was with a girl of about sixteen who, as I later learned, was his sister, and there was another girl whose age I wasn't able to determine at first glance. Ladi introduced me to her: "This is a friend of mine from class with the strange name of Thesar Lumi. He's a quiet guy and you'd almost think he was hanging onto a treasure so that the river didn't carry it away."

Ladi was obviously a bit drunk. This was the only explanation I could offer for his sudden interest in me. I wasn't surprised by the fact that he knew my name, although we'd never really met or spoken a word. He had also noticed that I was a quiet type, although I didn't see anything in that either. I was embarrassed like someone who gains the esteem of others because they've confused him with someone else. The frigid reaction of his companions made it clear that there was no question of esteem. The sixteen-year-old sister hardly looked up to greet me, and the whole time I was standing at their table – the whole time Ladi, with the vehemence of a drunk, tried to get me to sit down with them – she made no effort to hide her annoyance at my being there, as if I were responsible for her brother's inebriated state. Maybe, with the arrogance of girls of her social standing, she thought that I was unworthy of sitting with them. There's no need to go on any further about her because she plays no role in my story. But the other girl does, and I'll elaborate on her later.

As I said earlier, I wasn't able to guess her age right away. I'd have lost a bet with anyone who'd guessed she was ten years older than me. But she actually was ten years older. She had a child and had been widowed a year earlier. Her husband, an architect, had lost his life while he was

driving back from Durrës on a motorcycle with a compan-
ion, a fellow architect. The two of them were killed
instantly in an accident on the outskirts of Tirana. I was to
learn this later when Sonia, which was her name,
consumed me literally body and soul, and the two of them,
Ladi and Sonia, would form another constellation of pain
in the empty vaults of my existence. Sonia remained fixed
in my imagination the way I saw her that day: a pale face
with jet-black eyes, sensuous lips always slightly open and
revealing a row of even teeth; her thick, black hair, parted
on the side and falling onto her shoulders Whenever she
looked around, her hair covered half of her face, and she
had the self-confidence of a woman who was keenly aware
of her irresistible and overpowering charms. She was
dazzlingly beautiful. This might be the reason why I wasn't
able to guess her age and this was why I sat down and
stayed there to the very end, in spite of the snotty insults
from the sixteen-year-old. I was only interested in one
thing: watching that divine being called Sonia, sitting
across the table.

I was able to see her again three months later. I'd be
lying if I pretended I had forgotten her in the meantime.
But this was for the simple reason that she belonged to
another planet. She was unattainable. After an almost
sleepless night being bewitched by her femininity, I woke
up exhausted. I wasn't entirely unfamiliar with the sensation. I'd had my first experience with a girl the summer
before. Like many boys in my town, my first lessons in life
were taught to me by a gypsy girl. Her name was
Ermelinda, or Linda for short. She was seventeen and did
shift work at the cement factory. I'd just turned eighteen.
During the summer after exams, we'd kissed in the dark on
the road leading from the factory to her home, not far from
Sherif's house. Linda informed me from the start that I
wasn't an expert in kissing. The 'gadjo' boys, she mock-
ingly insisted, didn't know a thing about kissing and, in the
ways of love, they were no comparison to the gypsy boys.

Wounded to the core, I asked her why she was going out with me in the first place. She gave me a typically gypsy answer. It was because she liked my nose. She then took it upon herself to teach me the art of kissing. Several days later, she decided it was time to teach me something else: the art of love. I had told my parents that I'd be sleeping over at a friend's house and waited until Linda had left the third shift. We spent the night outdoors under a starry sky. By dawn I was worn out. Linda abandoned me in the bushes, planting a love bite on my chest. There were to be six of them in all, one for each night we'd spend making love. Just before she left, she whispered to me: "I knew you were a waste of time in sex." I fell asleep right away.

I was just as exhausted after the sleepless night I spent under the spell Sonia's eyes. It was as if an imaginary bite from her eyes had left a greater bruise than the six trophies I'd received from Linda. A light rain continued to fall, and it hadn't stopped since the previous afternoon. It was so quiet on the streets of our little town that I could hear the water flowing in the river. Looking up at the dark sky, I thought to myself that if the great Flood were to happen, Sonia would need to be among the survivors on Noah's Ark to perpetuate life on earth. I don't know if Ladi would have agreed with me. In any case, he was waiting on the stairs near the heavy doors to the faculty building with an umbrella in his hand. I didn't associate his being there with my arrival. But he was waiting for me, which was what he told me the minute we met. He spoke in a familiar way as if we'd known each other for years. He was pale. With the scarf wrapped around his neck, he reminded me of a little boy carefully following his parents' instructions. Ladi apologized to me. I had no idea why. Nothing had happened between the two of us which would have merited an apology. This was what I'd said to him and he laughed in his eternally sad way. He placed his hand on my shoulder, looked me in the eyes, and suggested that we skip class that day and go somewhere else. My only thought was that if we were going to Noah's Ark, we'd find Sonia there. But we didn't go to Noah's Ark. We went to the same café we'd been to the day before. And, of course, Sonia wasn't there.

This was how I got to know Ladi, or to be more precise, this was how Ladi got to know me. He was the one who took the initiative, not me, and he had the right to choose. My only right was to respond or not to his offer of friendship. I accepted it. To get rid of any misunderstanding, I feel it's important to explain that I responded to his offer without any ulterior motive. It never occurred to me and I had no desire whatsoever to profit from the social standing of his family. For quite a while when we were together, I had a guilty feeling because I didn't tell Ladi who I actually was. I was keeping one secret from him. If I had revealed my secret, it might have signalled an end to our friendship. To prevent another possible misunderstanding, I'm not trying to present myself as a saint. I had resolved not to let Ladi in on my secret, but it wasn't really out of fear that I'd lose his friendship, which might easily have happened. I was simply afraid of losing my identity. It would have meant my immediate downfall and I wasn't so naïve  as to be willing to sacrifice myself for reasons of ethics. At least that's what I thought. I was determined to go to my grave without revealing my secret, that is, if no one else discovered it first. I was mistaken, which proves that I didn't know who I was. But how can anyone really know who he is? Not long afterwards, with the greatest of ease, I told my secret – my biographical time bomb – to Ladi. And then to Sonia, too.

# 6

There was a snowfall at the end of January of the following year. The students went wild. The streets and sidewalks between the Faculty of Natural Sciences and the maternity ward were transformed into battlefields. Classes began an hour late because most of the students were unable to get across Scanderbeg Square, where chaos reigned. Ladi told me that it was his birthday. From the windows of the auditorium on the top floor we were watching the girls being pelted with snowballs. He asked me to come over to his house to celebrate the occasion. I was surprised. It was the first time he'd invited me.

Ladi looked unusually pale that day, and the casual way that he'd given me the invitation made it seem a bit inappropriate. I wasn't even able to thank him, but this wasn't because of the odd way he'd invited me or because of the paleness of his face. To my great fortune, the alarm bells started to ring on all the floors. The dean's office had obviously decided to intervene. Classes were scheduled to begin even though half of the students were still absent. We wandered off and took our seats near the door. The wind was blowing through one of the cracks in the window and Ladi wrapped his scarf tightly around his neck. I sat there for the whole lesson, with my elbows on the table and my head between my palms, and understood nothing at all. Ladi, for his part, was listening with rapt attention as if this were the most interesting lecture of all. On the way home, I told him the plain truth, without trying to explain it away or come up with an alibi. We shuffled down the centre of the road towards the downtown area – the sidewalks were too dangerous because of the snow and ice tumbling from the roofs – and there I revealed to Ladi the secret of my past – of the uncle who had fled the country. I was clear and concise about it, as if it was something quite normal, and used the same casual tone of voice he'd used to invite me over. Ladi was silent. In fact, the silence which reigned between us was quite logical. We continued walking into town. I'd imagined this scene while at the lecture, with my head between my hands. I'd figured that we'd walk downtown and then separate, both of us going our own, very different way. Ladi looked at me with his blue eyes. At that moment I solved a mystery that had been gnawing at me for some time, maybe since the day we got to know one another. Where had I seen his eyes before? They were Vilma's eyes – her glance transfixed in me. "Since it's the first time that you're coming over," said Ladi, "the guards won't know you, so I'll come out to pick you up at the bridge across from the Hotel Dajti at seven o'clock. Be on time, because I can't get away for long." He then shook my hand in his usual way and left without saying anything more. I stood there in the snow and mush until his silhouette disappeared behind the building of the puppet theatre.

I was waiting on the bridge across from the Hotel Dajti ten minutes before the appointed time. I hadn't been aware of how much Ladi's friendship meant to me. I'd never been so concerned about being on time for an appointment, and my nervousness while getting dressed proved to me that there was something sinister in my joy and anticipation. Yes, there was something that weighed heavily on me when I considered that I was about to cross a threshold which I never dreamed I'd cross. In my imagination, there was a whole new world on the other side, Ladi's world, so different from the one I lived in. I felt like Martin Eden in Jack London's novel, about to penetrate a mysterious environment, with the only difference that no Ruth was waiting for me, but a dour sixteen-year-old instead. As for Sonia, Ladi had presented her three months earlier as his cousin. As I waited at the edge of the bridge, I had no inkling that I'd see her again that evening. All I could remember from that rainy afternoon with Ladi and his sister was that I'd glimpsed a divine creation. I'd spent a sleepless night, and then the vision of her receded into the mist, as all memories do sooner or later.

Ladi arrived on time at seven o'clock. The boulevard was empty and there were hardly any vehicles going by the slush. Ladi looked just as pale as he had that morning, but it might have been the cold neon light that accented his paleness this time. He attempted to put on a good face. "I'm really looking forward to this evening," he said. "I just hope I'll be able to meet the expectations for a ceremonious event like this one. As for the guests, you'll get to know them yourself. I just want to give you one word of advice: say as little as possible and listen as much as possible. This way, I guarantee you'll have a good time. The guests will all be in a great mood and, since I'm the person with the birthday, I have to seem even more so. I'd advise you not to be too exuberant yourself. With all the nonsense you told me about earlier, we shouldn't be overly optimistic."

We passed the No Entry sign and the first two guards appeared, with the barrels of automatic rifles sticking out from under their capes. From here on the forbidden city began, a neighbourhood in town where the sidewalks, yards, gardens, pine trees, mimosas, privet hedges, and everything aside from the paved roads themselves were covered in a thick layer of snow. Untouched. In the corner of one yard stood a frozen snowman, like the ones you see in children's magazines. Everything was asleep, as if flicked by a magic wand. Passing a few houses of impeccable style, like the ones in architecture magazines, we turned into a side street which ended at a large two-storey mansion. With all the lights reflecting in the snow, it looked unreal. This was where Ladi lived. On the side of the road there was a black Mercedes with someone standing beside it. We walked through the wrought-iron gate into the garden, and the door opened. Two men came out at first, followed by Ladi's father. He was a tall man wearing a long coat and a rimmed cap. He came down the stairs, talking to one of the two men in civilian clothes behind him. He'd noticed we were there. But he only spoke to his son when he was right beside us, and didn't give me the slightest glance. The two men in civilian clothes were now outside the gate, waiting beside the Mercedes. The conversation between father and son lasted a couple of minutes. They were obviously having a disagreement. They spoke in low voices so that I wasn't able to hear what they were saying, but when they separated, the father seemed angry. He raised his voice and told his son that certain guests had to be invited. "That's an order," he declared, "no fooling around." Then he headed towards the car.

I had the impression of being treated like dirt. Ladi's father had ignored me completely. It would have been an elementary mark of courtesy at least to say 'good evening.' But, I remembered, insignificant people like me probably just have to accept the rules of the game. After all, it was honour enough for me to be in the forbidden city, a neighbourhood where even the air I was breathing was now different. We waited until the Mercedes drove away. It was obvious how upset and embarrassed Ladi was. He was as white as a sheet. I realized that I was far out of my depth. When we went into the house, Ladi left me in a room with a TV set in it. In those days, only two people in my native town had TV sets: Hulusi and Xhoda. I'd watched TV a couple of times at Hulusi's. Ladi asked me to wait there because he needed to make a phone call. It was obvious that the call had to do with the guests his father had talked about, and who Ladi was supposed to invite. Who could these people be, if a man as important as Ladi's father was so worried about them? The whole Party and Government elite was there that evening, the sons and daughters of the most powerful people in the country. They all looked so important, especially to someone like me. They arrived one by one, and in twos and threes. I couldn't distinguish which ones were the special guests who'd been invited at the last minute. They were all glowing and in a good mood as Ladi had predicted, but their exuberance didn't rub off on me. In spite of my friend's hospitality, I felt like a fish out of water. Ladi noticed my predicament. He laid his arm around my shoulders to show that I was his special guest and introduced me to everyone. It was a kind gesture, but it upset me even more. I felt like a monkey in a zoo being shown off to visitors. Ladi nevertheless continued to present me to the guests who were all very kind. I had no reason to think badly of them, but I just didn't feel comfortable. My conclusion was that it wasn't easy for someone raised on a dusty riverbank to overcome an inferiority complex. I'd heard that people with inferiority complexes have something fishy about them. In my case, I was envious of all the *jeunesse dorée* of the elite. When I realised this, I was more upset than ever and probably didn't make a good impression that evening. But maybe I'm just imagining things. None of the guests showed any special interest in me. Once Ladi had finished the introductions, I was consigned to general oblivion, forgotten and abandoned, even to some extent by Ladi. He was busy with the other guests and had no more time to spend with me. After a little while, I wanted to leave, but hung around anyway. Then Sonia unexpectedly turned up, and the world changed.

## 7

When I saw Sonia, I experienced what happens to people confined for a long time in the dark when suddenly the lights go on. I was standing in a hall which consisted of two separate rooms, with a sliding door between them. There were crystal chandeliers in both rooms. Along the walls at equal distances were oval side tables covered in sweets, fruit and drinks. Between the tables were chairs and stools, most of which had been empty when the lights went on for me. The guests, a good balance of young men and girls, were dancing. Loudspeakers had been placed at various locations so that the music, the soundtrack from *Love Story*, could be heard at any point in the room. Like the film and the novel, the song was a huge success that year and was being played several times a day on all the radio stations. Ladi had shown me a magazine with the main actors on the cover. I remembered their names. The role of Oliver was played by a good-looking guy called Ryan O'Neill, and Jenny was played by Ali McGraw. As I was saying, an orchestral version of the theme song of *Love Story* was blaring from the loudspeakers when the lights went on. I remember Sonia and I being at opposite ends of the room. Somehow we found ourselves together, surrounded by dancing couples, and most of them had their arms around each other. I also remember, when I saw her, thinking that she was much better-looking than the actress who played Jenny, and I whispered this into Sonia's ear. She smiled and confided that she didn't know who Jenny was, adding that it wasn't good for me to drink too much. I realised from this that I'd been drinking the whole time until the lights went on. "It was just as well," I thought to myself, "otherwise I'd have left long ago." I whispered this into Sonia's ear, too. She smiled again, and this gave me courage. "If I had left,"

I added, "I wouldn't have had a chance to let you know that none of these well-nourished girls are too pleased about your being here. Otherwise, they wouldn't have thrown themselves around their partners' necks, ready to be dragged across the floor." Sonia covered her mouth to keep herself from bursting out laughing. Either I was really funny or she was just pretending to laugh. I didn't care. Anyway, Sonia giggled at every joke I made and this gave me a lot of satisfaction. I didn't know at the time that my joy was being fed on someone else's downfall. I didn't realise while we were dancing among the couples that someone else's eyes were staring at us in anger. And I didn't know that this anger would spiral out of control. Sonia stayed with me all evening. She refused everyone else's come-ons and drank whisky only with me. We only danced when they were playing the blues. When at the end, in a carefree gesture to the rhythm, she obliterated the gulf which had separated us, I wasn't aware that someone else had flown into a rage and abandoned the party. At that moment, tasting total victory, Sonia let herself go, and I sensed inside me the instincts of a possessive male, and her hot breath on my cheeks and the glowing embers of her lips as they brushed and seared mine. But I didn't know the truth behind the joy which overpowered me.

Later on, Sonia tried several times to convince me that there was no connection between me and the fellow who was to be her victim that evening. I didn't understand why she was making such a big deal out of it. The more she insisted, the less convinced I was. I was touched by her mad desire to persuade me that she loved me, but it was a desire I'd come to see as ominous. I suspected it was an anticipation of bad luck that had caused her to become infatuated with me. Our relationship was in fact nothing more than an infatuation which was to last only for about a year. It seems that I was a bearer of doom. All those who have ever had a relationship with me have been plagued by misfortune. And yet, I was positive that fortune had found me in the figure of Sonia.

I'd never have believed that a woman with Sonia's overwhelming femininity would be susceptible to spontaneous compliments, but she was. She wanted to know more of who this Jenny was, if only to see whether my observations were right. "This Jenny seems like an attractive girl. But although I'm flattered to hear that you find me more attractive, I don't like to be compared to a dead person."

Was she serious or just joking? I raised my head, resting it on my elbow. She was lying on her back, covered by the sheets up to her shoulders. Her heavy black hair flowed thickly in my direction. I pushed it aside to get a better look at her. I thought my heart would stop beating. She was so unbelievably beautiful. I bent over and kissed her on the lips. She stretched and put her arms around my neck. The touch of her skin electrified me. I couldn't hold back any longer. She moaned at my movements until her muffled voice came out in short, feeble whimpers. She bit me on the neck as if to stop me. Then, as she turned her mouth away from my shoulder, she gave out a long gasp and cry, and pressed my face to her breasts. The fragrance of her skin penetrated my whole body and I collapsed. She writhed and grasped my hair between her fingers. Then she let go and threw her arms around my shoulders, lying there with her eyes closed.

"You shouldn't have made the comparison," she whispered. I was confused. Was she just kidding me? "I found the book and read it," she continued. "You probably haven't read it yourself. Can you read English?" she asked. I told her that I didn't know any foreign languages except the smattering of English I'd picked up at secondary school. She got out of bed and wrapped herself in her dressing gown. It was a Japanese kimono made of silk, the kind I'd seen once on TV. When she left the room, it occurred to me how absurd and undeserved this feeling of rapture was. Everything around me reinforced my happiness: the apartment, the bedroom, the double bed where, not too long ago, she'd slept with another man, her late husband. Oh God, I sighed, to die a senseless death and leave Sonia behind. Sonia reappeared in the room and interrupted my thoughts. She'd made coffee. As she was filling the cups, I mused that there was no reason to feel pity for Sonia's husband, all things considered. If he hadn't been killed, she'd have been unattainable for me, on another planet. Yes, my happiness was built on another man's tragedy, I reflected. Then I started to realise why Sonia didn't want to be compared to Jenny in the novel. She was superstitious. I told her earnestly that there was no more similarity between her and Jenny than there was between me and the son of a millionaire. Sonia didn't reply and I added: "Somehow it's obvious that you come from a ruling family."

Sonia pretended to smile which betrayed a hint of irony and derision. Her kimono revealed part of her breast. As she lay there trying to smile and sipping at her coffee, I cursed myself. Why, in God's name, had I started to talk about millionaires and prominent families? "I don't know why everyone assumes such a thing," she replied, while my eyes fixed on her breast. Her eyes caught mine as she sipped her coffee. Bemused, she looked down and then up at me again as if she couldn't believe her eyes. I blushed, and that's probably what saved me. Sonia put her cup to one side, took off her kimono and came closer. I was sitting on the edge of the bed. She held my head between her hands and clasped it to her breast. My lips moistened her tender skin. She quivered when I wrapped my tongue around her nipple, and pushed me away. Putting her gown on, she sat down where she'd been. I was still panting and lay back on the bed, covering myself with the sheets. To calm my nerves, Sonia brought me a glass of cognac which I guzzled. "You're a child, and a bit of a dimwit, too," she whispered. "So what makes you think that I'm from a ruling family? You know, I don't warm to people who think things like that. And, by the way, what do you mean by 'ruling family' in the first place? Do you think they're all like Ladi's?"

I stared at her, dumbfounded. I was never able to pin down Sonia and understand what type of person she really was. She could be flighty and sharp-witted, compassionate and cruel. Anyway, she was a bit of a libertine, in the most positive sense of the word. Compared to her, I felt like a fool. I couldn't understand how she'd managed to get me into bed just one week after our flirt at Ladi's birthday party when both of us had left drunk afterwards. "Just to make things clear, and to close the subject," she added, "I only went there because of Ladi. My father is a pretty stubborn guy. He only goes to see his brother, Ladi's father, if he has to return a visit. But this rarely happens. Is that clear?"

Very clear. I never broached the subject again, and neither did she. Although I was really curious to find out more about the great ruling families, I didn't want to run the risk of jeopardising my relationship with Sonia. I was sure of that, and had learned, too, that she was incorrigibly superstitious. Superstitious to the point of fatalism.

# 8

I'd loved to have strolled through the streets of Tirana with Sonia at my side and to have sat in the cafes with her. There's nothing that would have flattered my masculine ego more. But it wasn't possible, either for Sonia or for me. Sonia had plenty of reasons for keeping our liaison a secret. I had only one: that Ladi not find out. Sonia didn't tell Ladi either. Though we didn't exchange a word on the subject, I felt that she'd never have forgiven me if I'd given Ladi even the slightest inkling. My position was more difficult than hers. She wasn't obliged to Ladi for anything. But I was obliged to him for the friendship he'd offered me. I always felt like a hypocrite and a cheat when I was with him. This dichotomy weighed heavily on me. One day I almost blurted out the most idiotic thing to Sonia. I wanted to marry her. Now that things had spun out of control, I wonder if I'd have taken that crazy step – if I had proposed to her – whether things would at least have spun out of control differently. Sonia might have accepted and I'd have married her without the slightest hesitation. But with time, I turned into as much of an incorrigible fatalist as Sonia. I don't think I would have had the strength to channel things in another direction. Sonia would never have married me anyway. I was nothing but her lapdog. And that's the way she treated me.

The fever between us lasted for several months. Sonia seemed to be using me to prove to herself that there was no limit to human passions. Time stood still the moment we parted. Our surroundings lost their importance and we simply waited for the next day and the appointed time. I sneaked up the staircase to her fourth-floor apartment at the edge of the city centre where the door was left open for me. We spent hours in ecstasy. Sonia often arranged for her five-year-old son to sleep over at her parents' home, and I was then able to spend the night. These nights were of such erotic frenzy that I needed twenty-four hours of sleep and rest to recover from them. You could see the rapture in our eyes, especially in Sonia's. It was as though, in the shadow of impending doom, she didn't want to waste any time. She consumed me, body and soul. The time came when she insisted that I visit every day, and I did. Attending classes became a hassle and I gave no thought at all to the coming exams. One day, something happened which we had been careful to avoid. It happened in a most unexpected way, at least not as I had always feared it might. Catching someone in the act, so to speak, was quite a popular sport at the time. But who'd ever bother to spy on us just to catch us in the act? Well, someone did.

If there's one thing in my life I've always regretted, it's the fact that I didn't manage to give the person in question a thorough beating. After all, he was six inches shorter and so couldn't have been stronger than me. As for his age, he seemed to be about thirty, compared to my twenty. But, he was the son of a government minister, and this provided an incomparable advantage. When I told Sonia about the incident, she said: "That guy always meant two times nothing to me. It just happened that 'Two Times Nothing' was her appointed victim that evening at Ladi's birthday party. Sonia admitted to me that she had only gone in the first place to infuriate him. "That ass, he was after me while we were students. He came on to me within a week of my husband's death. I couldn't get rid of him, so I went to Ladi's party to show him that I'd go to bed with anyone rather than him. He's a monster."

I must have turned pale at that point in our conversation because Sonia fell silent. The expression on her face was like a child having a temper tantrum. She then felt obliged to reassure me that she loved me and would love me until the moment we separated, never to see each other again. To this day, I can't forgive myself for my meagre reaction. There are many ways in which pettiness reveals itself in a human spirit. I don't know what Sonia saw in my expression and I don't want to talk about it. What I saw in front of me was the 'Two Times Nothing'.

He was of average height, slightly balding and had grey eyes. The skin on his face shone, no doubt from an excess of vitamins or cosmetics. I noticed him at the foot of the stairs when I was leaving Sonia's building. I glanced to the left from force of habit, and passed him as he was leaning against a wall, smoking a cigarette. I didn't recognize the face. "Hey, it's funny you don't remember me," he called out when I was about ten paces away from the entrance. I looked at him with instant irritation, probably because I was exhausted. "Let me help you out. We met at Ladi's birthday party a few months ago. We even shook hands." I realised that I was mainly annoyed by his watery eyes. There was something sinister in his glance. A few minutes later, when I'd gone on my way, I changed my opinion. They were the eyes of a viper, welling with poison, and the poison was already circulating in my veins. He was succinct, decisive and absolutely clear. I wasn't surprised when Sonia later told me he worked as a police investigator and was the son of a powerful minister. He had spoken to me as if he were a police sergeant conducting an investigation. In spite of his doubts about my memory, I still know exactly what he had said, word for word: "Let's get down to business, and I'd advise you to listen carefully to what I'm about to say. You've been seeing a girl for quite a while now and you've just left her apartment. You're in a minefield. If you don't give her up immediately, I'm going to send two letters: one to Ladi and the other to the dean of the faculty. I'm going to tell Ladi that his best friend is sleeping with his cousin. The dean isn't interested in this, so I'll tell him something else which will probably be of interest to Ladi, too. If you don't do as I say, I'm going to tell the dean and Ladi that you have an uncle who fled the country, a fact that you tried to conceal and which doesn't figure on any of your documents. Have I made myself clear?"

I wandered through the streets, dazed. I was unnerved at the thought of his watery eyes and frustrated at the fact that I hadn't had the courage to slug him in the face. I'd thought of nothing else the whole time, and concluded that one good punch against his jaw would be enough to knock him out cold. I could hit him anywhere I wanted because he was quite a bit shorter and had to speak while looking up at me. But I didn't slug him. When he finished what he had to say, he turned and walked away. Maybe he suspected what I was thinking about. Maybe it was just a ploy to put me under even more pressure. In any case, I didn't have the courage to punch him. Instead I paced furiously through the streets until my confusion transformed itself into rage and frustration, if not to say naked fear.

I sneaked back to Sonia's that very night. I was used to sneaking in, but that time I really felt like a thief. I was afraid of those grey, watery eyes. Even if there really were no grey eyes, maybe there were eyes of another colour observing me from somewhere. But the result would have been the same. If they saw me, they'd transmit the message to the retinas of those grey eyes and the letters would be sent out in their respective directions. So, careful to avoid the glance of Grey Eyes, I tiptoed up the staircase to Sonia and told her everything, including my biographical 'time bomb'. As with Ladi, the time bomb made no particular impression on her. She informed me that Grey Eyes was extremely dangerous. "It has nothing to do with morals," she added. "Under the circumstances, you could be risking your whole future. We'll have to be very careful." Sonia thought it was more than likely that I'd be expelled from the university if my ticking time bomb were discovered. She wanted to avoid that at all costs. But she wanted me and I wanted her. We couldn't just dissipate into the atmosphere. That would have been the only way of escaping those grey eyes. Or to never meet again. But it was impossible for me not to see

Sonia anymore, and just as impossible for her not to see me. Not meeting each other for a day was like a century, a century in a person whose fear had suppressed all other interests. Our relationship soon became a passion filled with terror. Under those circumstances, both theoretically and practically, it wasn't possible for us to be cautious.

Doom appeared one day in the form of the little man I called Xhohu, my head of the department, that hybrid creature *sui generis* of Xhoda and Hulusi. Whenever I saw him, he reminded me of the expression that if you cross a snake and a hedgehog, you get barbed wire. It was no secret to anyone that Xhohu was the barbed wire of our department. I was surprised one evening when I saw Xhohu in a corner of Café Flora, chatting intimately with Two Times Nothing, the minister's son and investigator, A.P. They made a strange couple, the most unlikely one you would ever imagine in professional terms. One of them was the head of a university department and the other a cop. I was awake all night. There were lots of reasons which led me to believe that I was the subject of their private conversation. And I wasn't wrong.

The next day, after the first morning lesson, the secretary of the faculty caught me in the hallway and summoned me to the office. My heart started to pound. I hung around in the hallway until I'd convinced myself that I looked calm. Xhohu was alone. He was sitting in one of the armchairs, near a coffee table with a walnut veneer. I noticed an ashtray on it with a burning cigarette. Xhohu waved me in. I closed the door behind me and sat down in one of the chairs in front of him. Across the table drifted the reek of the bottle from a sour burp he had inadvertently let out. I felt like throwing up, but maybe it was more from his ostentatious behaviour. I understood in any case that I was trapped. To Xhohu's misfortune, he wasn't aware that I'd seen him the night before in a tête a tête with Grey Eyes. He tried without success to intimidate me with the grandeur of his presence. While I was waiting for him to throw the bomb, I mused that he looked, at the most, like a stuffed chimpanzee, like the ones children wind up with a key. The only difference was that he was being wound up by a cop. But Xhohu couldn't know my thoughts which gave me the opportunity to savour the aesthetics of the situation: an exemplary species of a subservient primate in action. Finally, taking a puff on his cigarette and exhaling a thick cloud of smoke, just as Two Times Nothing had done a while earlier, he came to the point: "It pains me, my good lad, to have to remind you that, in our society, nothing is considered more reprehensible than a lack of sincerity." He paused, staring at me to see what effect his words would have, and then carried on: "Personally, I do not have a bad impression of you as a student. And, on top of this, you are a good friend of Comrade Vladimir, and we both know who Comrade Vladimir is. This makes it all the more difficult for me to carry out the heavy responsibilities with which I have been charged. To put it briefly, consciously or not, you have committed a grievous act of deception. A citizen of your town has sent a letter to the dean's office informing us that you have an uncle who fled the country. The letter is anonymous but it was posted in the town you come from. We checked into the matter and discovered that the accusation is indeed true." Here he stopped again to take another puff on his cigarette. Seeing that he was having no effect on me, he continued in a harsher tone: "For the moment, the letter is in my safe, but I can't keep it there forever. I have to hand it over to the Party Secretary. From there it will go to the Committee. I imagine you realise the consequences. But I want to give you time until tomorrow. Perhaps you can find some miti-gating circumstances. Otherwise you are in deep trouble. Think carefully about the matter."

I was ready for anything, but I hadn't expected such a blatant form of blackmail. I was surprised that the minis-ter's son was such a weakling. He was giving me one last chance if I would only give up Sonia. He could destroy me, but he didn't want to do it because he was afraid. By destroying me, he'd lose his only opportunity of getting Sonia. But there was another reason, too. The nonsense about the anonymous letter showed that he preferred to stay in the shadows. The only person he had to be afraid of was Ladi because Ladi was Sonia's first cousin. As for Xhohu, in spite of all his huffing and puffing, he couldn't hide the fact that my deception had caused him substantial problems. With the story about the anonymous letter he was gambling, too, but his reluctance at getting too involved was more than obvious. Our knight of righteousness was riding between two fires and didn't want to get singed by either one of them.

I didn't know that my brain was capable of functioning with the cold logic of a machine. I didn't realise that I could be calculating. I kept Sonia out of the whole thing. Only Ladi could solve the mess, that is, if he might be willing to get involved. The streak of supreme sincerity within me had given me the courage to reveal my biographical time-bomb, and I was willing to come to terms with an even greater danger. It was the last part that posed the bigger risk. I would also have to expose my relationship with Sonia and then beg for his assistance. There was no other way out.

I went ahead in a completely shameless way, but in view of the mentality of my absurd surroundings, I had no other choice. I was a grain of sand, a nothing which anyone could trample on. Ladi would never leave me in the lurch, I suspected, and indeed he didn't. I have no idea what he thought. His pale face turned even paler. He sat there in silence as I emptied my sack of dirty deeds. Both the silence and the unusual paleness in his face indicated that he was very upset. But about what? About me? About Sonia? About Xhohu and the minister's son? Probably about the whole thing. We were small game, troublemakers and squabblers. On one of the rare occasions when alcohol got the better of him, he had told me how disgusted he was by the whole world. At those times he was overcome by self-destruction and it became apparent that a troubled spirit was hiding behind that composed façade. He had only one passion in his life: books. I've never met anyone who devoured books the way he did. Everything else was perfunctory, temporary, ephemeral. Maybe I was also one of the ephemeral passers-by in his life. That's how he viewed himself, too, as a passer-by.

It will always be a mystery as to how Ladi managed to solve the crisis in my life. A couple of days later he told me that no one would bother me anymore. My existence, very simply shaken to the quick, returned just as simply to its normal course. It was all very confusing. To save me, Ladi had no doubt made use of his father's authority. Both against Xhohu and Grey Eyes. I imagined how Xhohu would have squirmed. Ladi must have said something to him like: "Professor, you know that no anonymous letter was ever written, don't you?" And Xhohu would have answered: "There must have been some misunderstanding, Comrade Vladimir. I can assure you that no one wrote an anonymous letter." But what about the grey-eyed son of the minister? Ladi probably played the Sonia card, telling him for instance that if he ever bothered her again, he'd regret it for the rest of his life. He may have played another card, too. They came from the same circles and knew each other's weaknesses. As for me, I wasn't completely relieved. My biographical time-bomb, concealed for years, had now been discovered. If a policeman and Xhohu knew, everyone would learn about it sooner or later. I was uneasy for another reason, too. My relationship with Sonia was no longer a secret to Ladi. He was aware that I was going out with this cousin. I had no alibi for that. In a moment of childish naïvety, I resolved to put an end to things – I decided not to see Sonia anymore.

It was almost exam time. Ladi hadn't been attending classes for several weeks. I hadn't seen Sonia for at least ten days. Ten centuries. The world had lost its colours and was

back to black and white. I was unable to resist. I felt power-
less and wanted to escape, to live in a cave somewhere like
a hermit. But I was already enough of a hermit. There
couldn't be any escape.

I ran into Sonia on the boulevard. She was with me there
for about two minutes. Looking me in the eyes, she ordered
me to follow her. "Come on, right now, and pay attention
when you go up the stairs. You'll regret it forever if you
don't follow me." Then she turned and left. I was bewildered, almost crazy with happiness. I watched her, seized by
the idea of running after her, grabbing her and twirling her
around with me until the two of us were dizzy. The idea
remained constantly in my mind as I followed from a
distance which, to anyone with the slightest suspicions,
would have been more than obvious. I didn't care. They
could all see us. We arrived at her apartment at about the
same time. Sonia was pale as I locked the door behind me.
She wanted to say something, but I didn't give her an
opportunity, sealing her lips with mine. She resisted, whispering: "You're crazy." Then she devoured me. Her tongue
was on the attack, searching and sucking at my lips. I unbuttoned her blouse to discover she had nothing on under it.
She leapt at me, tearing off my clothes. I grasped her and,
sweeping her off her feet, groped my way to the bedroom.
Her hair swayed like the branches of a weeping willow. The
door was fortunately open. I laid her carefully on the bed,
as if she was made of glass, and nestled my face between her
breasts. I could feel her hands around me and her lips on
my neck. She moaned in agitation, her body in rhythmic
convulsions. Then she whimpered but, this time, her body
didn't come to a rest. She held me in a tight grip and kissed
me passionately as I penetrated her again from a different
position, the one she liked best. The pillow muffled her
groaning as the planet hurled itself into an abyss of ecstasy.
We kept it up until we were both totally exhausted.

"I should have hurled you out of the window. That's
what you deserve," she muttered. I lay on my stomach, my

hands cupped around one of her breasts. Her fingers stroked me gently and wove through my hair. "I'll throw you out of bed next time if you ever come back, sweep you down the stairs with a broom and slam the door behind you." I still had her breast in the palm of my hand and stroked her nipple. This usually pleased her when we finished making love, but this time she didn't react at all. She threatened me with other punishments, each one worse than the other, all of which I deserved in her opinion. Then she pushed me away. Supporting herself on her elbows, she told me she had found out everything. I froze. She threw herself at me and grasped my throat. "I'll strangle you, you traitor. Before going to Ladi, you should have come to me, coward! You've exposed us both, you egotist. I could have ironed the problem out much more easily than Ladi, you fool!" She spewed other epithets at me, with her hands still at my throat. I listened quietly without the slightest objection, and it turned out she was right. Just as suddenly as she had lunged at me, she turned away and broke into sobs in her pillow. I was bewildered, not knowing quite what to do. I stared at her quivering shoulders, her black hair flowing around me, and couldn't comprehend what this flood of pain and tears meant. Sonia was a passionate being, but she wasn't one for hysterics. Overcome by a profound sense of guilt and not daring to touch her, I begged her forgiveness, time and again.

Sonia got up and went to the bathroom, and came back in her kimono, with her breast still showing. She knew that this aggressive exposure of her breasts excited me, as a red flag would inflame a bull. She was well aware of this, but I didn't get the impression she was doing it deliberately. It wasn't the right moment, even though my eyes, out of force of habit, fixated on her chest.

She later calmed down and poured us each a glass of cognac. She said she had been unusually upset lately, but assured me that her tears had nothing to do with me. When I asked what it was about, she replied that the night before, her father, in a pleasantly tipsy mood, had gone out to pay a visit to his brother, Ladi's father, who unfortunately was home at the time. The two of them had had a fight. Sonia laughed, although I noticed a tiny tear escaping down her cheek. She revealed that her father argued with his brother every time they met. "You can't imagine all the accusations he made." She stared at me. "He called him a country squire, and that they were all acting like landed gentry. My uncle usually keeps his mouth shut because he's the younger brother, but this time, he chucked my father out. They might easily have arrested him. When he got home, still as drunk as ever, he kept ranting and raving at everyone. None of us got any sleep."

Sonia gulped down the rest of the cognac in her glass. She had now exchanged her dressing gown for a thin dress that, alas, excited me ten times more than the kimono. I stress the word "alas" because, in view of the mood she was in, she wouldn't have put up with any more of my advances. As if to make the point, she got up and wanted me to go into the kitchen with her for another drink. I agreed. After all, we were in her apartment, so nothing could go wrong. "The ruling families are the worst," she stammered. I was now sober and all ears. "They're disgusting," she continued, unconcerned about the impression her words were making on me. "There's only one decent person among them, and that's Ladi. All the rest are monsters. The men are crocodiles and the women are vipers. Not to mention the toads who try to hide their ugliness under thick layers of cosmetics. My father is right. Give me another."

I obligingly poured her another glass of cognac although I could see that she was already drunk. Sonia didn't tolerate alcohol well. To keep up with her, I gulped down another couple of glasses. I noticed it was getting dark outside. "Ladi doesn't get along well with his father either," she whispered to me. "They're like cats and dogs, but keep that to yourself. Don't tell anyone, okay? Let that be our secret." Sonia placed her hand around my neck. I bent over to kiss her on the lips. I don't know why, but when she mentioned poor Ladi, he reminded me of Hamlet. As we were kissing, I recalled the snowy evening of his birthday party, the fragments of the conversation he had had with his omnipotent father on the stairs of the mansion, his father's insistence that Ladi invite a few forgotten friends, who it seemed were all the more powerful.

We had another drink from the same glass and Sonia suggested quite casually that we go out for a walk. "They're going to see us," she added, "but frankly, I don't give a damn. The only one I didn't want to find out was Ladi, and you told him already. Are you afraid to go out with me?" "Of course not," I replied. I was on the point of falling to my knees and kissing her feet like a lowly page madly in love with his lady. At that moment, I refused to see that our relationship would no longer be passion but a declaration of war. The one to fling down the gauntlet was Sonia. I was inferior in this respect. My fighting spirit had dissipated long ago, the night in my childhood when I found out about my uncle, the moment my world turned black and white and I discovered it was composed of pedigrees and of mongrels. From that time on, my fight for survival seemed to exclude provocation. Sonia, on the other hand, proved that she possessed not only an aggressive femininity, but also another aggressive characteristic: pride. I now realise who Sonia was challenging. But at the time I understood nothing. I didn't know that she had declared war on all of her surroundings, which she would counter every step of the way with latent hostility. She had declared war on the elite. She never talked to me about this. I later understood why Sonia wanted to go out and be seen with me. But there may have been another reason. With her almost unbelievable insight, she saw the sudden end looming.

# 9

We met no one we knew on that evening when we first went out together, and none of the others living in the building saw us climb the stairs to her apartment. One problem came up the next day: my clothes. It was the end of May. The nights were cool and most people were wearing jackets. My clothing was modest and what escaped passers-by on the first evening of cognac-induced euphoria was noticed the next day. I looked pretty shabby next to Sonia, the epitome of sartorial elegance. I was painfully aware of the difference, and so was she. I forgot to mention that Sonia was an architect, as was her late husband. And one other thing: there were photos of him everywhere in the apartment, even on the night table beside the double bed where we always made love. He was a tallish guy, blond and good-looking, about thirty-five years old. At first, I was a bit embarrassed at him watching me. The first couple of times, I wanted to tell Sonia that I couldn't make love to her in his presence, but then I got used to it. If Sonia didn't mind, I'd have to put up with him, too. Sonia was a complicated woman and I was too much of a bore to understand the intricate aspects of her soul. I didn't even notice the similarities between the man in the picture and myself. She meant it when she swore that she loved me because when she looked me in the eyes, she was looking at him. I didn't understand at the time that when she decided to go out in public with me, as she used to do with her husband, she just wanted to be seen once more with him and prove to the world that she belonged to one person only. But maybe these are only the inventions and fantasies of a sick mind.

Be this as it may, Sonia was resolved to go out with me. Though no one spotted us on the first evening, that was soon to change. The second night we were both sober. She examined me from head to toe and said: "Let's see…" I followed her into the bedroom without saying a word, where she ordered me to undress. I took off my clothes. Impatiently she told me to take off my underwear, too. Then she went over to the dresser and took some shorts and a t-shirt out of a drawer. "Put that on," she commanded, and I obeyed. Then she found a blue shirt, a tie, socks and even an ironed handkerchief which had been in the dresser for God knows how long. She hesitated as she stood in front of the closet. I watched her movements like a curious child, ready and willing to fulfill all of her commands. She opened both of the closet doors, went through all the hangers, one by one, before finding me a pair of dark blue trousers. I put them on. They were just my size. I also put on a white jacket which was so light that I hardly noticed it on my shoulders. She muttered and then hurried to do up my tie and find me a pair of black shoes, size forty-two. They fit me perfectly. Finally, she shoved me towards the centre of the room and, stepping back, surveyed me in silent satisfaction. "Fine," she said. "Go and wait for me in the other room."

I had rarely been in her living room. I never felt at ease there. Here, more than anywhere else in the apartment, a person could sense the past – living proof that nothing had been changed. No one had the right to make himself at home in the absence of the owner. But the owner was in fact very much present. He was there with Sonia in a medium-sized photo on one of the book shelves. I went closer and picked it up.

"Oh God," I thought to myself, "to die at the height of your strength, at the zenith of your masculinity, to expire in vain and leave Sonia behind. How could such an awful thing have happened to him? Who deserved such a sense-less death?" "You," replied the man in the photograph, with a wide smile on his face. "If I were there, you wouldn't be." "Sparti was right," Sonia confirmed. "You wouldn't be around if he were still here. Either you or me, but not both of us." I was chastened to note that Sparti was wearing the same jacket and shirt, the same tie and dark blue trousers as I was, and probably the same underwear. The colour photo had been taken in the room where I was standing. They had been sitting on the sofa. I could now hear Sonia coming in from the bedroom so I put the photo back on the shelf and sat down on the sofa, quite accidentally where Sparti had once sat. When Sofia came into the room with the hues of a rosy-fingered dawn on her cheeks, I leaned against the backrest and could hardly keep from gasping my astonishment. She was wearing a mauve dress, and had a cardigan in her hand and a white handbag over her shoulder. The very same as in the photo. She stood in the doorway and it took a minute for me to think of getting up. I was almost sure that she was going to come over and sit down beside me, leaning her shoulder against mine, just like she had in the photo. Was it all coincidence or had Sonia staged everything on purpose? I didn't know because I wasn't yet really aware of my similarity to Sparti. And even if I had been, I probably wouldn't have mentioned it for one very good reason. By the time Sonia dressed me up in Sparti's clothes, she could do whatever she wanted with me. I was madly in love with her.

There was no doubt about it. Sonia was playing games and fulfilling some sort of fantasy. Otherwise there is no explanation for the fact that we went to the bar at the Hotel Dajti three nights in a row. Three nights and not four because on the third night, we ran into a certain police investigator, A.P., the son of the minister. From the start I'd noticed that Sonia wasn't exactly unknown here. I was the new boy, a surprise to everyone. The hotel manager, who we met in the lobby, the maître d'hôtel, all the other waiters, and even the band members in the tavern greeted her with respect, almost submissively. We sat down at a round table in one corner of the room to be as far as possible away from the band, but the noise was as deafening there as everywhere else. There were some foreign couples dancing when we came in. We ordered whisky and coffee. Sonia had given me a wad of money and asked me to take things easy and have fun. Having been raised in a little town on the banks of a river, I had some trouble acting the way she wanted, not to mention the fact that the tavern looked pretty dull to start with. The only things of interest were the foreigners, but they were busy among themselves.

Grey Eyes turned up at the tavern about an hour after we arrived. He was with a party of three, all of them wearing the same type of suit. The hotel manager showed them in. I saw them from a distance and my hand instinctively froze around my whisky glass. Sonia was chattering about the divorce of a friend of hers. The expression on my face must have changed, because she broke off her story, noticing I wasn't paying attention and was staring at the men standing at the entrance to the tavern. Sonia turned around to have a look and laughed. "You don't have to stare," she said. With an enigmatic smile on her face, she picked up her glass, gave a clink to mine, took a sip and set it back on the table. The newly arrived guests took their seats on the opposite side of the room. I lost sight of both them and the hotel manager. Sonia calmly returned to the story of her girlfriend's divorce, but then interrupted it again. The spotlights went out and the tavern was shrouded in a soft reddish light as the band began to play the blues. Sonia told me to drink up. She finished her glass, too. No one had been on the dance floor yet. "Come on," she said. There was no need for any further explanation, although I felt uneasy. I knew exactly what Sonia was after, who she was targeting and what signals she was sending. "Don't worry," she whispered. I told her she looked captivating and offered, if she wanted, to beat Grey Eyes to a pulp right in the middle of the tavern. "Don't bother," she replied, "he'll be furious enough as it is." Our solo on the dance floor was enough to attract the attention of even the most apathetic customer, not to mention the trio at the one table and the hotel manager, if he was still there. Other couples got up to dance and Sonia suggested we go back to our seats. The waiter brought more whisky, but Sonia had had enough. She ordered some roasted almonds, which were once the salty pride of the tavern of the Hotel Dajti. This was the most interesting thing I remember from the tavern that I've never set foot in since that time. I'd be interested to know whether the minister's son still patronises it.

"He noticed us in any case," said Sonia. "He'll be livid now. I've heard that he likes to torture his victims, the poor wretches who he gets to interrogate before trial. Everyone knows about him in Ladi's circles. There's a lot of talk, yet no one does anything. No one cares. Do you realize how many eyes are staring at us right now?" she inquired suddenly. "Don't worry. You're with me. For those guys, you being with me is like you being with Ladi. They're savages. In front of rabbits they play the tiger, but in front of tigers they play the rabbit." Sonia took my glass and had a sip. "This guy, though, is an upstart, just like his father, the minister. Do you know what I mean by an upstart? The whole government has fallen into their hands. Our whole, apparently so monolithic society, is rotten to the core because it's being run by upstarts. They're the great tragedy of the nation. It'll be difficult ever getting rid of them."

We stayed on for a while and then left. It was chilly outside. The main boulevard was empty. Sonja took my arm and we snuggled. I was actually on the verge of proposing to her, but I couldn't find the courage. I felt like an upstart myself, an upstart who, through a combination of luck and circumstance, had won himself a divine beauty.

Sonia's behaviour was growing more and more incomprehensible. According to social norms, she was creating a public scandal, and this is exactly what Ladi told her. We had just got out of bed and were having coffee when he phoned to say that he was coming over. I was in the midst of exam season. I didn't attend the first exam at all in order to give myself time to prepare for the second one. I hadn't seen Ladi for three weeks. "There's no point in you leaving," said Sonia. "He knows you're here anyway." Ladi showed no sign of surprise when he saw me. He told us that we'd been attracting attention, and that all of Tirana was talking. Then came the remark about a public scandal. Sonia laughed, something which unnerved me. I was no longer able to resist her whims. I had no particular desire to listen to their conversation, but Sonia would never have forgiven me if I had left. Under the circumstances, Ladi came to the point, stating that he'd come with an order from his father. Sonia was to pick up her son that very night, who she had left with her parents almost a month ago. She was supposed to be ready the next morning. A car would come around and take her and her son to a villa in Durrës for an as yet unspecified period of time. "A couple of months," said Ladi, "until you're feeling better. Father says you're suffering from a psychiatric condition. And he's not the only one who says so."

Sonia didn't laugh this time. She was pale. "Uncle can only order people around who are under his tutelage," she said. "I'm not and don't intend to be under his thumb. And as far as my health is concerned, I've never felt better." After she made her point, she left the room and came back with a bottle of cognac. She poured us each a drink and, as if to show us how it was done, swallowed hers in one gulp. Ladi didn't touch his glass, and neither nor did I. Sonia had the right to protest, but not in this way. That's at least what I thought, I who didn't know what rebellion was and who wasn't able to understand this woman. Ladi's face was paler than ever. "You'll do exactly as father has said," he ordered.

"I'm not kidding. And I don't have any time to waste. If you want to know the truth, father has definite information. If you keep on this way, something's going to happen to Sari (this is what he and Sonia called me). The secret we know is not a secret any longer. It's reached the ears of my

father and things look bad." Ladi fell silent and then turned
to Sonia again. "Don't be stubborn. There's no other way
out. Otherwise something's going to happen which even
my father is afraid of. He insists, and that's it! If you want
to hear my opinion, I think he's right. I don't know
anything more, except that father is really worried. I repeat:
worried, not angry. And, Sari, it would be better if you left
Tirana for a while. Go back to your town and get ready for
your exams there."

My thoughts went back once more to his birthday, the
evening with the snow, the conversation between father
and son, and his father's vehement demand that Ladi invite
only certain guests. It was clear to me that no one was safe.
Everyone lived in fear, no matter how powerful they were.
I could sense the fear in the way Ladi spoke, the way he
begged Sonia to obey. By now, I was petrified, too. A chill
went down my spine. I was the one who had caused Ladi
all the problems. "I'm sorry, so sorry," I stammered. Sonia
got up from the table and went over to the window. Ladi
sipped at his cognac and gave me a smile, as if to say:
"Don't worry, that's the way things are." When Sonia came
back, she had a tear in her eye. "Alright," she said to Ladi.
"I understand. Maybe I am ill and don't know it. Tell uncle
that I'll do as he says. But I can't leave tomorrow. Tell him
the day after. I'll be ready on the day after tomorrow in the
morning." Then she turned away. Ladi didn't react, but I
could see the relief in his eyes. He drank his cognac and got
up. "I'd better get going," he said. Sonia said nothing. Ladi
shrugged, shook my hand without a word, and went out.

I sat there in front of a full glass of cognac. I couldn't
even get up to see Ladi to the door. Sonia stood at the
window like a frozen statue. What was I supposed to do? I
decided it would be best to keep quiet. Finally, she came
over to me. It was a hot afternoon, and the cognac I had
been drinking made me even hotter. For the first time, I
admitted to myself that I didn't belong there. By sheer coincidence I had got myself involved in the lives of some

individuals who, although I was close to them, were surrounded by an enigmatic fog which I couldn't see through. Nevertheless, I had the impression that I understood Sonia better that evening than ever before. "Are you afraid to go out with me?" she asked. I reacted with the stupidest and most theatrical gesture of my entire life. I fell on my knees, grabbed her hand and smothered it in kisses. I had been to a western a few days earlier, and in this action-packed movie, the hero had knelt before his lover. As outdated as it may have been, I don't think that my gesture was completely inspired by the hero in the film. I just fell on my knees because they gave way under me the minute Sonia asked if I'd go out with her. It was obvious that it would be for the last time. This was also the reason why she had postponed her departure. Sonia didn't seem to see my sentimental gesture as excessive. She took my head between her hands and stroked my hair. Obviously, some acts which men regard as outdated are not seen in that light by women.

When it got dark, we went out, strolling glumly as if we were on the way to a funeral. Passers-by seemed to me like flies. I don't know what Sonia thought of them. We looked at each other when we got to Restaurant Donika. What better place to hide from curious eyes than at Donika's? Not only from Grey Eyes, but from others we hadn't noticed and probably wouldn't see that evening either. If anywhere, we'd feel at ease at Donika's. We lumbered up the staircase to the balcony in the restaurant where you had to be careful not to hit your head against the ceiling and sat down at a table in the corner. Across from us, near the railing, was an empty table with a direct view of the main part of the restaurant below. Sonia said nothing, and neither did I. Half an hour later, a waiter arrived to announce that they only had cabbage and meatballs. "Alright," replied Sonia, "two servings of cabbage and meatballs." "And beer," I added. "Sorry, we're out of beer," replied the waiter. "What do you have then?" I asked. "Only ouzo," he sneered. "Bring us two double ouzos, will you?" asked Sonia, interrupting his malicious gloat. It took quite a while for the waiter to return. By the time he got back, another couple had sat down at the table near the railing. At first, I gave them only a quick look. I had the impression they were engaged, and I felt sorry for them because there was nothing to be had but cabbage and meat-balls. And ouzo. That made me curious. Would the girl at the other table drink the ouzo? Then I noticed she was staring at me.

If there was one person I hadn't counted on seeing in that restaurant, it was Vilma. She was there with her cousin, the guy who had helped me to discover what food Max preferred. She blushed, probably because I had caught her staring, and turned away. I knew she was attending a secondary school in Tirana and was close to graduation. Her father was still headmaster of the elementary school at home. I felt compelled to watch her and was sure that she'd sooner or later look back. Not to look at me, but to size up Sonia. I wasn't mistaken. She soon made one of those random movements of the head, typical of curious high school girls, to have a good look in our direction. She wasn't prepared for my trap and fell right into it. I had to laugh, in spite of the terrible sadness of that evening. She blushed from ear to ear. "What a fool I am," I thought to myself. Sonia then suggested that we leave. The waiter hadn't come back for a full half hour, so we took off.

# 10

It was a boring summer. More than boring, it was a complete waste of time. More than a waste of time, it was a complete void. I wrote my autumn exam at the end of August. It was the time of year when pressure systems from Africa invade the country to prove that autumn had no intention of showing up early. Ladi returned to class two weeks late. I was still longing for Sonia when I met him, but neither of us mentioned her name. Ladi had no reason to and I didn't dare to. "What absurd conventions," I thought. They spent the whole summer together. He probably just left her two days ago, and yet I had to keep my mouth shut. That frustrated me and I got angry. I wanted to tell him that I hated customs like that, that I couldn't care less what people thought, and would go and visit Sonia that very night, even if I had to fight off half of Tirana to get there. It's painful to think back on that time. Of course, I said nothing. Even today, the ache of remorse still gnaws at me. Ladi was teetering on the edge of an abyss and I was only thinking of myself. But how could I have known that he was in such a predicament?

Everything dragged on as usual. Mount Dajti loomed above the capital in eternal Olympic serenity. Ladi's eyes were sad as always and his face was pale. How was I to know that an earthquake was about to erupt? I was no prophet. I was just a poor guy dying of lust to sleep with Sonia. An upstart, as Sonia called them. I was an upstart in love. Things which had no connection with Sonia didn't interest me. I couldn't foresee that under the swamp a fire was raging which would soon bring all the toads and tadpoles, eels and snakes to a boil. My thoughts didn't reach that far. No one could foresee what was going to happen, except the ones who could already feel the heat under the soles of their feet. I was nothing more than a piece of kindling placed beside a blazing log, and together we would burn.

I met Ladi in mid-September and noticed he was now a little absent-minded. It was still hot out. Everyone complained that the schools hadn't closed down for the heat wave, and wandered around in a daze from morning to night. I don't know if Ladi could feel the fire burning under his feet. If not, it wasn't far off. No doubt under his father's armchair. Blinded by egotism, I had no idea the world was spinning out of control around me. The two months without Sonia had made me oversensitive. I interpreted everything – every event and act – in relation to her, especially anything Ladi said or did. My brain was producing erroneous data, like a computer infected with a virus. I interpreted Ladi's depression as a cooling off towards me, his habit of avoiding people as an attempt to avoid me, his not wanting to go out for a drink as a strategy not to be seen with me, and the exclusion of Sonia as a plot against me. Then came the day in early October when I noticed how petty he'd become. "If you're interested," said Ladi after a lecture, "come out to the Kisha restaurant on the outskirts of town this evening. I'll bring some whisky." This was right after he had turned down my invitation twice to go out with him. "Sorry," I replied in a tone which betrayed a slight dissatisfaction, "I'm afraid I'm busy." Ladi pretended not to notice. "It's too bad you can't come," he countered. "Sonia's going to think I forgot to tell you." After that very casual remark, he changed the subject, asking me when we'd have the next colloquium with Xhohu. I told him that it was scheduled for the following week. Then we took off. He down the main boulevard and I headed towards the street leading to the travel agency, where my bus stop was. My heart was pounding like mad. I couldn't hold out any longer. Turning around, I shouted to him in the distance: "Hey, but bring a full bottle this time." He waved. I spied a rare smile on his face. Then he was gone.

This would be the last evening together for the three of us. It would also be the last time I slept with Sonia. They say that if a man finds out the moment of his death, he'll dig his grave with his own hands. I'm convinced that neither Ladi nor Sonia knew what was in store for them. There was no way they could know, and neither could I. The outing itself went well. We drank a whole bottle of whisky, as well as wine and beer. The staff made us some delicious hors d'oeuvres. Not because of Sonia though. Alas, people tend to submit to power, not to beauty. The waiters and cooks at the little restaurant on the lake were no exception. Sonia's beautiful eyes were of little significance to them. If it had only been a question of beauty, they probably would have let me starve. But not Ladi, because he had power, and power is a much bigger attraction than female beauty. Power fascinates everyone, men and women. Men strive for it to the point of perversion and women long for it to the point of losing their femininity. It was a fact that no one at the lakeside restaurant that evening, not even the waiters and cooks, knew what was in store for my companions. And I didn't know what was waiting for me.

Later, after events had taken their course, I heard rumours that the first signs of the insanity of that winter had been noticeable for quite a while, and were more than obvious at the end of the year. For instance, people had noticed during the New Years festivities that the portrait of Ladi's father was missing from the ones of all the high Party officials. Their images generally decorated the streets of the capital on occasions like that. Most people denied this, insisting they had seen his portrait there with the others as usual. But even if it had been missing, I wouldn't have noticed it. Portraits of officials were the last thing that interested me. I didn't read newspapers, with the exception of obligatory articles read out at public meetings and which were considered to be important for some reason. There was another thing I did notice in the following months: Ladi had lost his interest in books. His absolute priority in life had always been reading, whereas now he was wasting his time with me in bars. This was the period when Sonia broke off all contacts with me. If I hadn't had Ladi's companionship to keep me going, I'd probably have committed some irreversible error. For this reason, I didn't pay any particular attention to the change in Ladi's behaviour. For me, he had simply adapted to my desperate situation after the loss of Sonia and, in my egotism, I took this as a sign of solidarity.

I heard from my father about the first rumours circulating in town. I was studying for my last exam of the season, scheduled for the end of January, when he came into my room. He was pale and could hardly stand on his feet. And he was stuttering. My father stuttered whenever he was worried about something. According to rumour, Ladi's father had been declared an enemy of the people two or three days earlier and had been sent to prison. No one knew why. A number of other people, of various degrees of notoriety, had also been relieved of their posts. More arrests were expected. Father was so upset about what had happened, that it took a lot of effort for me to understand what he was saying. He started to pace back and forth, whining and cursing, but didn't have the courage to name names. He was petrified, particularly because Ladi had been to our house a couple of times and father had boasted to the neighbours that his boy was a good friend of the son of a powerful figure. Now, he was terrified and didn't know what to do. "We're finished," he stammered. "That's all we needed! Why did you get involved with him in the first place? Didn't we have enough problems already? God, what have you done to us?"

I left him to whine and went out. Otherwise, we'd have punched each other. I didn't know where to go. My head was bursting. It was a chilly January day. The trees were bare and the roads were empty. The town was waiting to be engulfed by another long winter night. What importance could events in the capital city have here? Who cared about official portraits or the absence of them? It was fed up with that kind of gossip. Our town was more worried about fist fights in local bars, and about knives being drawn without warning in some guys' drunken stupor. The portraits which were put up or taken down provided nothing more than material for jokes. The more courageous observers said things like: 'I hope they bash one another's heads in'. The portraits themselves, as they were being put up and taken down, had no idea that the citizens were treating them with supreme indifference.

The town was so deathly still that day that you could hear the water flowing in the river. The freezing wind chilled me to the bone. Only then did I start to understand what my father had said. The specific events had apparently taken place two or three days earlier. I broke out in a cold sweat. Ten minutes later I was standing in the filthy hall of the PTT where there was always someone arguing with the telephone operators. I put a coin in one of the phones and dialled Ladi's number. I let it ring for quite a while until I was convinced that no one was going to answer, and plunked the receiver back on the hook. The machine spit the coin out. I tried again five minutes later. I must have tried fifteen times at eight p.m. when the building was full of people coming and going, but there was still no answer.

I went home. Father had managed to terrify mother, too, and they were waiting for me when I got back. Mother's eyes were swollen. I was furious. I wanted to scream and tell them to leave me alone, but instead I went to my room without saying a word, and left them standing in the hallway. They definitely understood that any attempt to talk to me would be futile. I threw myself on the bed, but got up right away, as if ejected from the mattress by a broken spring. My parents were still in the hallway. As I ran down the dark staircase I heard them begging me to come back. When I was outside, I wasn't sure whether the noise in my ears was being caused by the river or by a pounding in my skull. I got off the bus at the stop near the travel agency and hurried to Sonia's apartment. In the dim stairwell I heard a woman whisper to me that Sonia wasn't home. She was at her father's place. When I turned around, the woman was gone. "I'm going crazy," I thought. "I'm getting hallucinations." But Sonia wasn't there. With almost idiotic perseverance I rang the bell loudly over and over, but no one answered.

I can't say what time it was, and I don't remember how long I sat at the bottom of the stairwell. The night air chilled my bones, so finally I got up, afraid that I'd fall asleep there on the staircase. No, Sonia wasn't at home. The voice I had heard was no hallucination. Without waiting any longer, I headed northwards, and trudged the one kilometre to the neighbourhood where Sonia's parents lived. The streets were empty. I walked, listening to the noise of my own steps. I wasn't sure exactly what I wanted and even why I was going in that direction. Now I couldn't help wondering whether I should have gone in the first place. Then I wouldn't have seen how small people can become, how weak and insignificant. That's also exactly how I felt when I got to the street where Sonia's parents lived: small, weak and insignificant.

I noticed the car from a distance the second I turned into the street. Only the parking lights were on, as if during an aerial attack. Maybe that's what caught my eye. A car with its parking lights on was unusual. I slowed down. I could hear voices whispering and see people moving around silently. Then I noticed the police standing on the sidewalk beside a vehicle, a large Skoda truck with a covered loading space at the back, and a trailer. I saw it all as if through a veil of fog, though not from the cold, although it was chilly enough outside. I realised they were being sent into internment. My knees began to wobble. An instinct of self-preservation nailed me to the spot. The street was plunged into darkness. The neon lights were out and curtains were drawn in all the surrounding windows. However, the slight movement of the curtains revealed that the neighbours were watching. I got close enough to hear the voices. Then I saw Sonia, who was carrying her son in her arms. Behind her was her father and, behind him, her mother. There was a big commotion in the stairwell. People were bringing things out and loading them into the trailer. The truck itself was already full. She stood there on the sidewalk on the opposite side of the road. A couple of steps and I could have been beside her, but I stayed put and bit my finger until it started to bleed. Sonia was so near, but I didn't dare show myself. I stayed in the dark, like a mole. A man dressed in civilian clothes came out from behind the trailer and went over to Sonia. It was him, the minister's son. Sonia turned away. If I hadn't been sure that I couldn't be seen by anyone from my position in the shadows, I'd have believed that Sonia saw me. She stared into the dark, trying to avoid those grey eyes. She couldn't know that there was someone in the dark. I clasped my hands behind my head and was on the point of banging it against the wall. I couldn't hear what the police investigator A.P. said to Sonia, or what she replied. When I looked up again, they had started loading the whole family into the truck, and with them was Sonia. The vehicle drove off a few minutes later. Curtains were still swaying in the windows. Go away, all of you, I wanted to shout. There's nothing but shit on this earth. I am shit and so are all of you! And we deserve to be treated like shit.

It was sunrise when I got back to my hometown. The buses were sleeping, too, so I had to walk home. Sonia's weary eyes and her empty stare into the void had cut me to the quick. Maybe that was the reason I could feel no other pain. I slept like a log. When I woke up, the world was drained of its colours. I had the feeling of being plunged into eternal darkness, and everything that took place afterwards left me cold.

Nothing special happened, only what was to be expected. I didn't show up for my exam, not only because I hadn't opened a single book for a long time, but also because I didn't want to give in to illusions. What did surprise me when I discovered it, was the incredible degree of human iniquity. I noticed it from the start of lectures. No one sat or came near me. I took a sick delight in seeing how the masses of students had been turned into beasts driven by their instincts. A person can't reproach a beast for being a beast, because it has no conscience of its own. In fact, I was quietly expecting something else, which happened later. On the second day of lectures, the student spokesman came up to me with unconcealed disgust, as if he were touching something unclean, and informed me that I was to report to the faculty office. There was no one there when I arrived except the secretary. She was a tall woman with glasses and attractive legs, apparently much to the envy of the female students. It was obvious that she felt very awkward. To encourage her, I smiled, which caused her to blush like a little girl. Her behaviour and her voice were also just like a young girl's. "I am sorry to inform you," she began, "I hope you will understand. I don't know why I was chosen to tell you, because it is not my job. Anyway, they have asked me to inform you that, as of today, you may no longer attend classes because of some- thing in your past which has come to light, which is... incompatible with your presence here at the faculty. I am so sorry. I was asked to transmit this unpleasant matter to your attention although it is not really my job. I know how difficult it is for you and I would like to assure you of my sympathy and respect..."

I wanted to tell her she looked like an angel, that she didn't belong in that sordid office but in heaven above, that she was a siren from paradise, but I couldn't get a word out of my mouth. Maybe I was able to express my gratitude in my expression. I'm not sure. I didn't know if she was able to read other peoples' expressions through her glasses. At any rate, I replied with a placidity bordering on cynicism that I could only accept her verbal communication as being official if I were given it in writing, signed and sealed. Otherwise I didn't see any reason to interrupt my studies. She hesitated. "Of course," she replied, "this is your right."

I left the office and went back to class. I knew my resistance would be useless. A decision had been taken. In the most cruel way, I'd already lost the two people I cared for most, lost all trace of them, without them having harmed anyone. Once more I called to mind that snowy night of Ladi's birthday, the conversation between father and son, the father's insistence that a certain individual or individuals be invited to the party. Ladi hadn't complied with his father's demand, I thought, as I remembered staring at the professor's somniferous gestures. Whether they were invited or not, they were furious and probably said to themselves: "Look at that consumptive snout-face who dares to insult us. We'll chop off his head and throw it to the pigs with all of his kith and kin." And then the chopping began. The first to roll, according to rank, was the head of the family. If he still had his head on. Mine would be next, I thought to myself in horror. Someone tapped me on the shoulder. It was the student spokesman. Again with evident disgust, he told me in a whisper to report to Xhohu, right away. Right then, I had the distinct impression that I was going to be decapitated.

Xhohu showed me in without any formalities. I knew what was going to happen. Before he started, I was about to tell him he didn't belong in that office – swept and cleaned every day and electrically heated – but somewhere in the seventh circle of hell. Xhohu, for his part, without gracing me with so much as a glance, began with the following declaration: "If the gentleman insists on having everything in writing, he shall have it with no problem at all. But not from us. We do not have such things in writing. They are issued at the office of an acquaintance of yours, a certain A.P. If my words do not suffice, I am afraid you will have to report to A.P., where the matter can be dealt with, in writing…"

Xhohu's words were more than convincing. I hadn't anticipated this turn of events. I left the office shaking from head to toe. Xhohu's warning was crystal-clear, and there was nothing I could do about it. I took off fast, running like a beaten hound dog, like the ones they throw stones at. Like some mangy mongrel.

Seeing the vomit between my feet just made me want to
throw up again. My muscles knotted into a cramp and I
banged my head against the trunk of the pine tree. There
was nothing left in me but bitter gall cascading into the
pool of gastric mucus, mixed with surrogate coffee and
cognac. "Get out of here, you lunatic!" I repeated in my
daze. "What are you after? The one you're looking for is
under the earth. Tragic sphinx, she's long gone. Nothing
more than a pile of bones under the soil. But the two of us,
you and I, are still here, damned to torture each other until
time immemorial. You're crazy and I'm lost. Who was the
luckier of us here on earth, you fool? I can see what
happened to you, I've known your fate for years. But with
those bloodshot eyes of yours, can you see what's
happened to me? Go away. Nobody's going to invade your
abandoned house. Go on in and get some sleep. Maybe
you'll have a nice dream. I had a dream last night. I saw her
fleeing over the waves of the sea. She was wearing a white
dress, like a bride's gown. I mean, she was dressed like a
bride, but she looked just as much like a child. I cried
because she departed with the refugees. What does the
dream mean, you lunatic? And why last night?"

"The lunatic will never give me an answer," I thought.
I managed to wrench myself from the trunk of the pine
tree. The sun had discovered a gap in the dirty grey of the
sky and sent down a ray of light to earth. Blinded, I stumbled along the sidewalk. Xhoda stayed on his side of the
fence, sitting on a chair and with an iron bar in his hand.
In front of me, Arsen Mjalti's snack bar appeared. The
door was open. It had been closed just a while ago and
now, all of a sudden, it was wide open. That meant there
was a way of alleviating my overwhelming urge to cry. If I

didn't drink, I'd be in tears. And I went into Arsen Mjalti's snack bar. Who cared if he made his meatballs with dog meat. I couldn't get through the day, under that grey sky, without a drink. But, as opposed to Xhoda, I knew she was no longer among the refugees. She was in the breast of the cold earth, in the form of a pile of bones. Where was the Grim Reaper to seize the two of us left behind here? Let's eat Arsen Mjalti's shit and drink his urine. This by no means derogatory sentence rang in my ears as I staggered into the snack bar, inhaling the thick smoke of cigarettes mixed with the fumes of fried meatballs. Of course, seeing the aggressive expression on the normally complacent face of the snack bar owner, I was convinced that none of us left behind would get anything to eat and drink. I was handed a portion of meatballs wrapped in a piece of paper and sprinkled with salt and pepper, and a large glass of raki, and took my seat in a corner of the bar, with one hand holding my ribs. I devoured the meatballs as quickly as I could, but savoured the raki slowly. If it had been cognac, I'd have gulped it down. I was really thirsty – so much so, that I'd have poured a whole glass down my throat, just like truck drivers do when they pour water into their over-heated motors. But I kept taking little sips, slowly and patiently. This was the only way of quenching my thirst with raki. And of getting rid of ominous thoughts. I thought for a minute of grabbing the glass and pouring the raki down the ex-foreman's throat. I had the impression that the raki was of an even more dubious quality than his notorious meatballs. But instead of carrying out my dastardly plan, I continued to sip slowly at my glass and even ordered a second one. My need was fulfilled instantly. I don't remember how long we exchanged platitudes, Arsen Mjalti and I. When I left, the sky was low and dark. There were flashes of lightning over the hills on the other side of the river, and a couple of drops of rain splashed onto my face. I looked around. The square was empty. A bus stopped, but no one got off. It was as empty as the square. I stood all alone and watched the bus disappear slowly into the distance. The town, sleeping the sleep of the dead, was about to ride out a storm. I walked for a bit, but my knees were wobbly. They didn't have the strength to keep a drunk on his feet. My only wish was to get home as quickly as possible...

# 11

"To get home, and as quickly as possible," I thought. The bus had left and no one got off. The square was empty, the sky was low, a February sky: cold and dirty. Hostile, like the expression on Xhohu's face. I was still tormented by his threat. 'If you would prefer it in writing…' Of course I didn't want anything in writing. I'd have to report to Grey Eyes and, from what I'd heard, he took particular delight in torturing his clients. I didn't want to become a client of Grey Eyes. My parents had the same opinion when I told them about my encounter with the God of the faculty. Mother tore at her hair and father started to pace around the kitchen. This time, it was my father who calmed the situation down, and very simply. Having paced back and forth several times, he stood still for a minute and said to my mother: "Stop whining. No one's been killed. We're just having a streak of bad luck". Then he turned to me, and added: "Just forget it. You did what you had to do. Look towards the future. If you hide, as you usually do, you'll get sick. What I mean is, it doesn't bother us if you hang around here and do nothing for a while." Thus spoke my father, and went out and made us all a cup of coffee. Strangely enough, he didn't betray any fear this time. I was the one who was terrified, and I'm not ashamed to admit it. The disappearance of my friends, and Xhohu baring his teeth had petrified me. If I fell into the clutches of Grey Eyes, who knows what would happen to me! So it was more out of fear than following my father's advice that I decided to take a job at the cement factory, as a labourer in the limestone-crushing sector. Grey Eyes forgot about me. When I started work, I realised what was behind his indulgence. The factory was hell on earth. Yes, I'd entered hell myself, without being dispatched there by him. The personnel division didn't need any special instructions. My CV was quite sufficient. My uncle had fled the country and, on top of this, I had been a good friend of the son of a certain person. That was more than enough for people to get goose bumps at the very sight of me. As to my expulsion from university, a horned devil like me was unworthy to study. A horned devil like me was only worthy of hell on earth, the cement factory of our town which produced more dust than it ever did cement.

One devil never harms another. The five devils in the limestone crushing sector, six including me, were hospitable enough. There were three gypsies and two gadjos. My arrival rectified the imbalance. The minute I showed up, a Skoda truck arrived with a trailer full of limestone to be unloaded and crushed. This served as an opportunity for me to show my credentials. I was exhausted when we were finished. I looked over at the others who had taken their seats in various corners and were eating quietly, and thought to myself that, if I continued working like that, I'd be dead by the end of the week. But I didn't die. Not at the end of the week, or at the end of the month, or at the end of four months. I might have been dead though, if I'd kept it up beyond four months. My colleagues, limestone-crushing devils that they were, assured me from the start that no one had ever died at the crusher, or at any time in the history of the whole pulvirulent factory. I wanted to protest that this was no wonder. The factory was hell itself, and mortals, when they die, are sent to hell to atone for their sins for all eternity. But I said nothing, not so much out of fear, but, as simple people, I didn't think they'd understand my reasoning. They were such sinners and had already died. I didn't want to remind them too much of this. But they insisted that they had been resuscitated from death and hell. Three of them, two gypsies and one gadjo, had been sentenced to various lengths of time in prison for theft and were 'ordinary' prisoners. None of them believed they'd spend much time at the limestone crusher. Having survived hell, they thought of the job as purgatory on the road to heaven, but they didn't elaborate on their vision of paradise. They were a happy group of limestone-crushing devils, optimistic and usually in good spirits. I say 'group', but in this assembly of low-lifes, five of them, six counting me, there were in actual fact three clans. The first one was made up of the optimistic ordinaries. The second consisted of one person, a gypsy of around thirty years old, a former bus conductor, who'd been sentenced to one year on probation after a fight. The third clan also consisted of one man. He was in his fifties and had been there for two years since his release from prison, where he'd served a ten-year sentence for anti-government agitation and propaganda. One thing was clear to me from the start. Every time we finished discharging and crushing a truckload of limestone, the optimists withdrew to one corner, the former bus conductor to his, and the political detainee to another. This constituted something of a problem for me. Which clan should I join? The solution was simple. I kept away from all of them. The optimists would no doubt have welcomed me, as I could see from their friendly smiles. But they were too curious and I didn't like that. So I decided to reciprocate only with a friendly smile of my own. The former bus conductor thought of himself as better than everyone else and was unapproachable. He was wary of the optimists because he saw them as informers. And he didn't want anything to do with the political detainee, thinking of his own year on probation as the appropriate sanction for his manly crime. The only problem was, I didn't warm to him as a person. He ate a lot, several times a day, probably to show off his exorbitant wealth as a former bus conductor. The only one left was the political detainee. I didn't learn much at all about him in the course of the four months we worked together. He was a surly, chain-smoking type who didn't talk much. I tried speaking to him on several occasions but with no success. Each time he sent me packing with a weary look that told me to mind my own business. I decided to form my own clan, consisting of me alone. We were six men in four clans. Clans of sinners, mortal sinners.

The work day started when we assembled at the hut near the crusher. The first truckload didn't usually arrive before eight so that we had a bit of time to warm ourselves at one of the ovens fired with corn stalks. The optimists were really pesky with their vociferous stories of erotic adventures, but there was nothing that could be done about it. There were three of them, and they were all young and strongly-built. No one dared to oppose them. As for the one-time conductor, he vented his frustration by sitting down and tucking into his food. The more the optimists shouted and laughed, the more he'd stuff himself. The detainee, who was not only a chain-smoker but also extremely sensitive to the cold, would get as close as he could to the oven. He always had a glum look on his face. Whenever the optimists shouted, he'd wince, gnash his teeth and give the impression that he was ready to lunge at their throats. Nothing ever happened though. The poor guy sighed and turned towards the open doorway to stare at the thick clouds of smoke billowing out of the factory chimney. The column of smoke rose vertically and then widened to form a dark mass which covered the river valley like a kerchief. It settled slowly and uniformly over everything, a black kerchief as if the town were in mourning. The optimists kept on with their erotic jesting, the conductor muttered, and the detainee withdrew into his own grief. I observed them all from my corner of the hut and imagined Sonia with her hair tied in a black kerchief, a kerchief of smoke and dust. The smoke and dust of hell. Where was she now? Somewhere. I wondered what had happened to her and Ladi, lost who knew where and abandoned forever. They were so far away from me and the hut that I shared with five other men, divided into the four clans.

Suddenly we could hear the screech of the Skoda, and in the doorway stood our God, lord on high over six men in four clans. This was the foreman Y.Z., who thundered and cursed louder than Zeus on Olympus. We were indifferent to the mischief of the gods on Olympus. We had our own Little Zeus who supervised and checked up on us, and twice a month he'd fill out the payroll list with our names. Beside each one he'd inscribe a symbolic sum of money. Then we would duly add our equally symbolic signatures. The trucks thundered in and Little Zeus turned up at the entrance to the hut almost at the same time, with mechanical precision. This precision reminded me of a Pavlovian experiment with dogs that we'd done at school. The subject was conditional and unconditional reflexes and it was carried out as follows: the dogs were given their food when they heard a bell ring. When the food appeared, they'd start to secrete saliva. Later on, the sound of the bell alone was sufficient for them to secrete the saliva. In our case, we learned to jump to our feet the minute we heard the truck. The noise signified that Little Zeus would appear at the doorway and we'd then start the process of crushing several tonnes of limestone. The appearance of Little Zeus also caused the temporary dissolution of the four clans. The six devils were instantly transformed into the superbly coordinated limbs of a beast. In synchronised movements, the lime-crushing beast leapt onto the trucks and trailers, hurling chunks of lime down to the factory floor. Then it lunged at the piles of rock, gasping, panting, six-fold sweating, emitting six different odours of sweat merged into one. Added to that was dust, cement and coal, blocking all its six-fold pores. When the crushing process was finished, Little Zeus disappeared, and the six-legged beast fell apart. The clans were formed again, each of them receding to its own corner of the hut to catch its breath, wash off its sweat, and rest. Calls of nature were always answered outdoors, and never in the toilets, because their stench was unbearable, even for the shortest of visits. The optimists returned to their effusive erotic bantering, the conductor opened his lunch bag with voracity, the detainee went back to his usual depression, and I stared at the billows of black smoke and thought about my lost friends. Then suddenly the roar of the truck could be heard again and, equally suddenly, Little Zeus materialised in the doorway. So it went, day in, day out, all with mechanical precision – exhausting, monotonous and fiendish.

It occurred to me for the first time that there was somehow always a solution to be had, even when you realise that you've been transformed from a human being into an animal. When you reach the animal stage, the stage of being nothing at all seems preferable. I'd turned into a beast and it was better to be nothing than to be an animal. Physical exhaustion makes you more predisposed to the idea of extinction. Earlier in my life, Sherif's father used to annihilate the mongrels in the streets with the help of a hunk of liver. He'd even had a piece of lamb liver left over for Max. The idea of physical extinction by means of a piece of liver fascinated me. I'd seen it happen, quickly and without too much pain. There was quivering, a few spasms, foam at the mouth and droopy eyelids. And then nothing, eternity. Or maybe rebirth in another form of existence. Ladi had driven me up the wall a whole night long once with the theory of a Japanese philosopher, whose name I can't recall. According to him, after death, life resumes in a new form, the soul takes root in a new being, or in a tree, for instance. Possibly in a dog. If this were true, I'd certainly end up as a street dog with a hunk of liver from Sherif's father. I had no big wish to test the theory of the Japanese philosopher. Not so much out of fear that I'd actually be reincarnated as a mongrel roaming the streets, but just because I didn't have the courage. You obviously had to be a bit Japanese. They thrust swords into their guts and commit hara-kiri at the drop of a hat. No, I wasn't Japanese and didn't believe in the theory. But if you don't believe in anything, you live in fear, fear of a million different things. You are paralysed, terrified of the unknown. But maybe it was sheer chance that prevented me from testing the theory of the Japanese philosopher.

It was a nice day in April. I hadn't slept a wink the night before. I couldn't even get to sleep in the early hours of the morning, as I usually did after a sleepless night. I got dressed mechanically and went out, and didn't feel either the cold or the warmth. Either my body wasn't reacting or it wasn't able to analyse external stimuli in order to determine whether it was hot or cold out. I knew it was Sunday and saw it was a beautiful April morning. One thought obsessed me as I wandered down to the riverbank, and that was whether the fish in the river suffered from the cold. If they were cold now, how would they have survived the winter? Since they could all swim, I reasoned that they probably kept themselves warm by swimming around. I couldn't swim. If I fell in the water, I'd freeze because I wouldn't know how to swim around like a fish and keep myself warm. Then I thought of Sonia. She probably knew how to swim. Assuming she were standing on the riverbank and her son fell into the water, how could she save him if she didn't know how to swim? But she could swim, and I couldn't. That's the reason why we never had fluvial or maritime discussions.

The river flowed silently. Its water was sparkling clear. Without taking my shoes off, I leapt over a ford and landed on the other bank. A part of the river and the hill behind it were hidden in fog. I followed a path towards the foggy side of the hill. "That's why the sky is so clear," I thought. "The clouds have broken up and descended into patches of fog." At the end of the hill, the river broadened into a loop and formed a lagoon. There were quite a few lagoons along the river. They would form and then disappear. This particular one was always there, caught between the hill and a sandbank which was only submerged when there was flooding. The lagoon was deep, and the fish, little and big, seemed to love it. So did the fishermen. The guys in town, being impatient, liked to fish using a type of soft explosive known as Turkish delight. The story went around that one particularly naïve boy, when he heard about the fishermen's success, actually started using the candy as bait instead of worms. The others told him that the fish loved it. Since that time, the fishermen have disappeared from the lagoon. With all the Turkish delight and the high sugar content in the water, the fish started getting diabetes and died out. Talk about 'fish brain'! If fish could talk, they'd curse one another as 'human brain'. A true fish brain couldn't imagine anything as perverse as the human brain.

I'd emerged from the mist and could see the slope of the hill and the lagoon between it and the sandbank. Everything was deathly still. I changed directions and headed for the top, where a cliff descended into the lagoon. It was here that the bravest young guys would dive into the water. Of course, this was only in the summer when the beach was full. Now there was no one there, just me hiking up to the promontory in my soggy shoes, without really knowing where I was going on that clear April Sunday. My legs carried me mechanically up the hill. To put it in the language of sports broadcasting, my ascent transformed itself into a virtual flight. But as I wasn't a bird and had no wings, my flight would be more like a freefall. There would be a huge splash in the lagoon, which would frighten the little fish if there were any left. And I didn't know how to swim. My legs propelled me up the hill until I got to where I was going.

First, I stared down at the surface of the water. I was getting dizzy and would probably have fallen off the cliff if I hadn't stepped back. It was an instinctive reaction and made me chuckle. I realized that I was suffering from vertigo. I always got dizzy at heights. My body doesn't like them. I laughed because I had no Japanese blood. But my legs were still on the move and made me rise to my feet and approach the cliff side again. Once more I was dizzy. The surface of the lagoon was rippled down below. I started to feel rippled myself, and suddenly got the impression I could fly and make a soft landing, as if on a thick layer of cotton. As I stood there, wavering between my desire and my aversion to fly, I noticed a couple of people down at the edge of the sandbank. All of a sudden I was gripped by the fear of falling. I stayed put. If I had moved another inch, I would have plunged into the abyss. The people were staring at me and I was staring at them. Vilma later told me that she'd screamed when she saw me, because it was so obvious that I intended to jump. "I was only relieved when I saw you sit down at the edge of the cliff. Father called me silly because I screamed. But that was because I recognised you. I was terrified you would fall. Father just made jokes. He said the air up there would be good for your brain."

I recognised them, too. That we all happened to be there at the same time can only be seen as an act of providence. A fatal act, although I didn't jump. I sat down, covered my face and broke into a sob, not knowing why I was sobbing. I couldn't foresee the repercussions of this encounter. If I'd been a prophet and glimpsed the two of them standing on the edge of the sandbank, I would have jumped. Into eternity, into nothing. But I wasn't a prophet. I had no talent for predicting the future. I probably collapsed in tears because my vision of flight lost its magic the moment I saw them. They'd come out to go fishing, Vilma with her blue eyes and Xhoda the Lunatic, who wasn't yet completely insane. I sobbed, not knowing what the future had in store. I certainly wasn't a prophet.

# 12

A person can get used to being treated like an animal very easily. It's no coincidence that human beings are known as the most adaptable of creatures. After the failure of my freefall on that sunny April day, everything became simple, as if by magic. My only objective was survival, in any form and under any conditions. Survival to see the light of day, to breathe the air, to eat, to satisfy bodily needs. Survival to comprehend my own inferiority, to understand the scorn of the privileged, of the people who, to their good fortune, didn't have an uncle who'd fled abroad or a friend who was the son of someone or other. Survival simply to survive. In cases like that, a chunk of bread is more than enough for the receiver to praise the Lord seven times a day. I didn't praise the Lord. I didn't believe in him. I preferred to praise Little Zeus, our brigade foreman, Y.Z., lord over six devils in four clans. Life becomes hard where there are devils and clans, even if they are peaceful devils, and kind and generous clans. In my case, the devils weren't particularly peaceful, and the clans weren't overly generous. A huge uproar happened every day over insignificant details, which were blown out of all proportion. It wasn't long before the optimists set their sights on me. They took particular pleasure in it, maybe because I'd been a university student. Maybe my alleged deeds had become known and were being talked about. Maybe, with the sort of instinct men like that have, they sensed that I was an easier victim than the former bus conductor or the political prisoner. In any case, they set their sights on me with incredible vindictiveness. They came from the capital and naturally thought they were superior, but they forgot that I was from a little, working-class town. A guy from a town like that, even if he's a former university student, may have many weaknesses, but he at least knows how to hold his own in fistfights and knifings. I was too proud to seek help from the friends of my childhood. Most of them were unemployed, hung around in the streets all day, embellished themselves with knives and other accessories, and would easily have been in a position to drive the thugs from the big city out of town. I didn't ask for their help, and I didn't want it. It may sound ridiculous, but the reason for this was that Fagu was still the head of the gang, the same Fagu I'd known as a boy. A lot of water had flowed under the bridge. We'd seen each other in town and had exchanged glances, and knew that nothing had changed in our relations. Rather than seek assistance from his gang in town, I chose to make use, if you will, of Little Zeus, the foreman. He'd been able to straighten those thugs out and without the use of force. A word from him would be enough to have their toil at the limestone crusher extended by six months. Little Zeus was from my town and knew the ropes. He helped me, so it was him that I praised.

My confrontation with the optimists led to an occurrence I hadn't foreseen. Neither Little Zeus nor I were in a position to impede it. This was the sudden re-appearance of Linda, the gypsy girl Ermelinda who'd put an end to my virginity. Linda worked a mere fifty metres away from us, at the same job in the cement mill where she'd been two years earlier. I crossed her path the first day I showed up for work. She smiled and gave me a wink. Nothing more. The fact that she didn't speak to me didn't offend me. I had other things to worry about. I later learned that she was having an affair with the foreman of her shift. He was jealous to the point of insanity, not of his wife, but of Linda. He would beat her for no reason at all, so she avoided creating any misunderstandings. I learned something else which I hadn't known earlier when we were going out together, although everyone else seemed to be well informed about it. Only her mother was a gypsy. Her father was white. He was the manager of the concrete-mixing sector and had been a crane operator at the time Linda was conceived. This explained the pale milk-chocolatey colour of her complexion. I discovered this from the optimists, the source of all gossip. Linda's name often cropped up in their lurid conversations but none of them dared to go near her. The foreman of the shift would have taught them a quick lesson. Guys like that sensed danger just as a wild animal would. They knew when to cower and when they could bare their teeth. On rare occasions they'd make some comment when she passed, but Linda didn't deign to turn around or speak to them.

I was perplexed when Linda came to me. It was mid-May and prematurely hot out for that time of year. The beaches in Durrës were said to be packed already. When we'd finished processing a few tonnes of limestone, the six-legged beast fell apart, and each of the men receded to his corner while waiting for the next truckload to arrive. Linda made her appearance at the entrance to the hut, and looked around in the most casual way. The former bus conductor froze with a lunch bag in his hand, and so did the political prisoner with a cigarette between his fingers. More baffled than the others were the optimists. She said, word for word: "Hey, Sari, could you come out for a minute?" No one ever called me Sari there. They usually called me by my proper name. When they wanted to make fun of me, the optimists would call me Thesi. Only two people had ever called me Sari: Sonia and Ladi. After she spoke, she disappeared before the others had time to collect their thoughts. She was waiting for me outside, about thirty steps away, out in the sunlight, and was covered from head to toe in cement dust. I could only see part of her face from under the bonnet, and her thick overalls concealed the contours of her body. Just as succinctly as she'd called me, she declared: "Meet you tonight at eight at the usual spot" and left. I froze under the sun, staring at her swaying thighs. Anyone else under a bonnet and overalls like that would have looked like a dusty scarecrow. I knew what was hiding behind that scarecrow who'd captivated me once again with her glance. She'd summoned me as if we'd just made love the night before. It bothered me that she had no doubt whatsoever that I'd obey her. I went back to the hut, where the optimists shot a couple of barbs in my direction. I ignored them because I didn't understand what they were getting at. Fortunately, a new truckload of limestone thundered in just then, and Little Zeus loomed in front of us. We clambered to our feet and reconstituted the six-legged beast which started crushing the rocks, without Little Zeus having to use his whip. Linda's voice and the word 'Sari' echoed in my ears, but I could make no sense of it. Now just a simple component of the six-legged beast, I was searching for something else, for the meaning of my existence.

"I called you Sari so that it would sound familiar and so that the others wouldn't suspect anything," explained Linda when I asked her where she'd got the nickname. When I insisted on knowing why she'd used that term and no other, she grinned. "The alternative would have been Thesi," she added, "but it wouldn't have sounded very affectionate." A compelling argument. The optimists would have given Linda full points on that one, if they'd been around. We lay in a close embrace, though more because it was a cool evening, if not to say cold, and Linda wasn't heavily dressed. She seemed to feel the cold more than I did and hugged me tightly to keep warm. Maybe also to warm me. She was hot, and I was ice-cold. Linda seemed uneasy about my frigidity: "I'm going to give him the brush-off," she whispered, drawing me close to her breast. "I never loved him. The only one I ever loved was you. I only went out with him to avoid having to work the night shift. You don't know what the night shift is like. I haven't been on it for a year now. But now that you're back, who cares!"

Linda unbuttoned my shirt. In her childish naïvety, she was worried that I'd be upset about the foreman. I'd come to meet her only because we hadn't had an opportunity to talk to each other. Linda's protest was superfluous because

I didn't care one bit about her affair with the foreman. But she insisted and was so full of pain and anguish that I felt sorry for her. I stroked her head and pulled her towards me. She lunged at me passionately. Her body emitted a musky fragrance and, for a minute, with Linda in my arms, I thought of Sonia. Linda twitched and Sonia writhed. Linda gasped and Sonia moaned. I took off her blouse. Her hot breasts pressed against my chest. My body was frozen. I was horrified, ashamed and embarrassed. I couldn't make love to her. Not because I didn't want to. My chilly reaction had a name. Did Linda understand? She did everything she could to excite me until she touched the block of ice. She withdrew her hand immediately as if she'd touched hot iron, and stared at me in the dark. Her eyes were like a cat's. Then she turned away. In the pale moonlight I could see tears dripping down her cheeks. Linda didn't understand a thing. She cried, not knowing the reason for my chilly reaction. She thought I didn't love her, not realising that I wanted her but wasn't able to make love to her. She then calmed down and her breathing returned to normal. It was the chill of the night air which sedated her. She put her blouse on and buttoned it up pensively. She didn't leave immediately, and she didn't pronounce sentence right away. Then it came: "You're impotent!" she hissed angrily and left. I stayed there in the dark. Linda had understood.

The optimists were in an aggressive mood the next morning. If they'd known what had happened between Linda and me, their mood would have been quite different. But they had no reason to suspect I'd gone out with Linda. The filthy bastards wanted to get back at me because their pride had been injured when Linda came by to see me. I wasn't in a peaceful mood either. Their constant attempts to taunt me had reached the breaking point. It seemed like a good day for settling accounts. For quite a while now I'd been carrying a knife on a chain, stashed in a pocket of my trousers. I'd bought it from a gypsy when it became obvious that there would be no end to the provocations of the optimists. It was a nice knife, with the shiny steel blade of a bayonet. I'd never used it, not that I was reticent to do so, but only because the opportunity had never come up. It all happened in a flash. Their leader, who was about twenty-five years old, was smaller than I was. As we were waiting for the truck to arrive, he turned up his nose, sniffed and said to his buddies: "Smells like a bag of shit here. How can you stand this guy? He smells like shit." I leapt to my feet and gave him an unexpected punch which hurled him to the ground. The other two, one white and one gypsy, threw themselves at me. We battled our way out the door. All I remember is that the gypsy at one point lay sprawled on the ground with a bleeding nose. I received a head injury, and gravel spewed in all directions. I learned later that I'd been knocked out by an iron bar. Fortunately, no one had noticed the knife in my pocket, not even the orderlies who tended to my wounds. The former bus conductor and the political prisoner gave evidence in my favour. They'd had enough of the optimists, too. But the incident didn't come to trial. When I got back to work after two weeks' sick leave, the optimists were gone. Little Zeus had sent them packing to the brick factory where they were happy. All in all, they'd been lucky not to get several months in prison. The leader of the gang managed to convince them that I'd started the fight. Little Zeus asked me if my head was still aching. I said no. He then sat down beside me and brushed the leg of my trousers with the back of his hand. "What do you need that for?" he asked. "Those guys knew all the time that you had a knife. They even told me where you kept it. I believed them when they told me about it and that you'd slugged them first. But you know, anyone who goes knifing is likely to get knifed in return." Nevertheless, I didn't divest myself of the knife for as long as I was in the realm of Little Zeus. I just hid it in a different pocket.

It looked at that time as if Lady Luck was once again stretching her hand in my direction. And I took it. I'd not yet come to realise how perfidious she was. I'd not yet understood that every time she offered me her hand, it soon turned into a shattering fist. When Lady Luck stretched her hand out this time, I threw away my knife. Had I known what was in store for me, I'd have sliced her hand off.

# 13

Not Dori's hand. I refuse to believe that Lady Luck extended her hand in the form of Dori's. That year, he was chief engineer at the plant and, because he had the reputation of being an excellent professional, he was appointed to rehabilitate that prehistoric monster, the cement factory. Certainly no blessing. Dori was four or, at the most, five years older than me. I remembered him from school. The smaller pupils usually remember the bigger ones, but it rarely happens the other way around. Nevertheless, Dori remembered me. He came over to me one day in the tavern. I'd just started sipping at a drink at an isolated table in a corner of the long, narrow premises, where I would later become a regular. On the other side of the room was Fagu's crowd. Most of them were out of work. I kept my distance from them although they invited me over from time to time. Fagu looked askance at me from a distance. He was employed as a mechanic at the plant. I don't know what hours he worked, or if in fact he ever did. He seemed to spend much of his time in the tavern and, when he wasn't there, he was to be found in the shade of the pine trees outside with his companions. There they would observe passers-by, taunt the mentally deficient and whistle at the girls. But not all the girls. Only those who didn't have a protective, knife-bearing brother or cousin.

I was sipping at my cognac when Dori came over. He had a glass of the same in his hand. He was a short, husky guy who was beginning to turn bald, and had just got engaged for the first time. I had seen him once in a while with his fiancée boarding the bus for Tirana. I wouldn't have been surprised if one of Fagu's friends had come over to my table. Not all of them, of course, because not all of them had the courage to be seen with me. But Dori was the chief engineer, a specialist, and it wasn't seen as proper for a specialist to associate with the likes of me. For this reason, I was quite surprised and bewildered when he came over with a glass in his hand. More confused than anything. At first I associated his appearance with the incident which had taken place between me and the optimists. The conversation we'd had did have something to do with an incident, but fortunately not the incident involving me. One of the girls in the laboratory had disappeared. Maybe it was the hand of Fate. The girl had taken off with a truck driver to Fier or Vlora or somewhere, and so a new job became available for me. I didn't have to think twice. I didn't thank Fate, but instead thanked Dori who'd offered me the position, and who actually begged me to take it. In view of the sorry state of my body, ravaged by my current job, the laboratory post seemed like paradise. Dori told me to come around to the management office the next morning. From there, with his help, it'd be a straight road to heaven. I'd no longer have to put up with the thundering of Little Zeus, or the sheer exhaustion of keeping that monster of a limestone crusher fed. My poor bones would find peace and quiet. I thought about everything, both about the political prisoner who'd be crushing limestone until he was crushed himself and about the former bus conductor and the optimists. There was only one thing I didn't imagine at the time: that I was about to run into Vilma at the laboratory.

Of course, I knew that Vilma worked in the lab. I'd seen her coming out of the plant dressed in white overalls, a white jacket and always with a white bonnet on her head. I'd seen her from a distance. In the hellish environment I worked in, her brief appearance proved to me that somewhere in the surrounding area there was a world different from the one I was putting up with every day amongst the satanic faces of devils. Compared to the wretches of that hell, she was like a divine apparition. It was maybe for this reason I thought I had a ticket to paradise when Dori convinced me that, as a student in his second year of industrial chemistry, I was just the right man to fill the position of the laboratory assistant who'd disappeared. In reality, paradise turned out to be a boring room with boring equipment which made deafening noises day and night. To put it in a nutshell, it was nothing at all like paradise. The only real change in my life was that, when I began work in the lab, I didn't have to take my lunch with me wrapped in newspaper. I was no longer toiling among devils. Instead, I was to spend my days in the company of two human beings dressed from head to toe in white, one of which was Vilma.

Before Fate led me to Vilma's lab, it took me to an office where there was no dust and no noise. The lighting was not too strong or too weak and the one window was covered with iron bars. To get in, you had to knock on a sheet-metal door coated with white enamel. The second you opened it, you found yourself in a cage, with iron bars rising on both sides from the floor to the ceiling. It was like being in a prison cell. But it was no cell, it was the personnel office. Inside the iron cage was an employee surrounded by shelves and safes. I'd been to his office a few months earlier when I started work in the brigade. The same guy was there, with a broken electric heater at his feet. In an office like this, he must be a prisoner, I thought when I saw him. The employee, who was bent over a desk which was piled with documents, would have chuckled and sniggered at me if he could have read my thoughts. Then he'd have guffawed, pounded on the safes with his fists, and screamed in my face: "You people are the prisoners here: I have all of you locked up here in my safes!" Whether he could read my thoughts or not, he made no move to pound on the safes. He'd only have injured his hands and he wasn't quite that stupid. The employee raised his head from the documents and told me that I was to start work the following day at the laboratory, on orders from management. This 'on orders from management' he stressed several times. "I had a dozen candidates for the job," he sniffed, looking me up and down as if to see what was so special about me. "Here, take this," he said, handing me a piece of paper with my appointment to the laboratory, on orders from the management of the cement factory. When I stretched out my hand to get the paper, he suddenly took it back. "Let me remind you, boy, that nothing has changed for you," he muttered, almost spitting at me. "The limestone crusher is waiting for you. It is exactly where you left it, and I don't think it is going to move." With this, he gave me the paper, and I backed out of the iron cage as if with my hand full of spit. He'd turned his back on me. I was overcome by a feeling of disgust, and fled.

"Yes," I thought, "nothing's changed for me, and it won't ever change." And yet, Lady Luck took me by the hand and led me off to the laboratory. Vilma was there, sitting in a chair, minus her bonnet. I honestly wondered if this was really Xhoda's daughter I saw in front of me. I had goose bumps. I saw Ladi's eyes in her face, just as I'd once seen her eyes in Ladi's. Vilma smiled and I had a lump in my throat. I wanted to cry. Here they were, Ladi's eyes. But it was Vilma, not Ladi. This didn't mean that he didn't exist. He was somewhere. But where? And under what circumstances? "Don't smile," I wanted to say to her. "I'm the same person I was and will always be the same. I haven't changed and never will." I grinned, which Vilma interpreted as a reaction to her smile. If she'd looked at me attentively and been able to read my eyes, she'd have understood that the expression on my face was anything but a smile and had nothing to do with hers. Vilma couldn't know that right then my confused brain was reciting the words of a poet who'd recently been sanctioned severely for a stanza which was something to the effect of: "I am the person I never was, I will be the person I am not". They made mincemeat of the poor devil for his blasphemy. For my part, they were turning my life into a living hell. There was no other explanation for the admonishment of the employee in the cage. The words 'What's up, tiger?'

popped into my brain and I had to laugh. Vilma invited me to take a seat. I had the impression that a tiger was listening to our conversation from behind the door. Wallowing in the azure of her eyes, I decided to keep my distance. A tiger was following my every footstep, a tiger that might consume Vilma, just as it already had Ladi and Sonia. I didn't want it to gobble up Vilma, too.

As much as I tried my best to keep my distance from Vilma, we were breathing the same air for hours on end in a room where the maximum distance between us was never more than six metres. I say maximum distance because we usually had to work less than one metre from each other and I could feel her breath. If the clanging and rattling of the cement mill had ever stopped, I'd have been able to hear her heart beating. But the noise and rattling never stopped, day or night. I couldn't hear her heart beating, but I was a participant in our endless conversations on topics of Vilma's choice. She had no interest in the tiger. Maybe she didn't even know the tiger existed. I'd have preferred that she keep quiet. The tiger was there, and it was listening. It was in the broken window pane which let the dust in, in the dark corners of the room and in the cracks in the walls. I knew it existed, I sensed its presence, and I could smell its feline stench and the stench of death it brought with it. A chill ran down my spine. My feet were stiff and heavy. I couldn't get my mouth to open.

Vilma was the child she'd always been and still had that immature insistence to get her own way whenever she wanted. What she wanted was to invite me to lunch in the canteen. I'd made excuses ninety-nine times, but the hundredth time I wasn't able to refuse. You can't say no to a child forever.

In actual fact we didn't go alone. There were three of us. Wherever she went, Vilma took Lulu with her. Lulu was the other assistant in the lab, an old-maid type. A maid no doubt from the virginity point of view, but not really old in the sense of real age. She was only about twenty-five, but with her thin, slightly hunched body and the sad expression on her face with its piercing eyes, she was more like an old lady. She'd grown up in an orphanage. From the start, I understood two things about her. Since she had no family of her own, Lulu regarded Vilma as part of her existence and worshipped her to the point of submission. Her love for Vilma was like the love of a dog for its master. I also came to realise that, like all faithful dogs, she was fiercely jealous and attempted to protect Vilma from everyone she considered a threat. At first, Lulu's hostility towards me proved to me that she saw me in the threat category. The hostility eventually let up. The savage glance in her eyes became more neutral until one day there was even a glimmer of friendship in them. Vilma may have tried to conceal her moods, but it was impossible. It wasn't only her childish behaviour that betrayed her but, more than anything else, Lulu's eyes. They were a mirror where I could always see what was going on in Vilma's mind. I could see when she was confused and could recognize anguish. When Lulu's eyes started to glow unexpectedly one day, I had to think of Max. Remembering the agony he must have gone through, I couldn't find any reason not to accept Vilma's hundredth invitation to have lunch with them in the canteen, even though the tiger was waiting for us outside as well as in the canteen. The tiger was lurking everywhere. But we had Lulu with us.

We were at the canteen for the third or fourth time one day when Fagu came in. His being there wouldn't have had any special significance to me if I hadn't noticed signs of alarm in my two companions' expressions. We were sitting in the middle of the room. Fagu was a few tables away from us. He'd strolled in with his hands in his pockets and a scowl on his face. When he went by us, he intentionally knocked over a jug of water with his elbow, and it shattered on the floor with a huge clatter. That was how he attracted the attention he was looking for. It was quiet in the canteen and all heads were turned in the direction of the noise. It was obvious that he intended to provoke all the workers on their lunch break, he sat down at an empty table a few metres away from us. Either something had gotten into him or he'd just come out of a cowboy movie, I thought. I drank up my wine. When I set my glass back on the table, I noticed that Vilma had gone as pale as a ghost. Lulu was watching me with trepidation. Oh God, I thought, what's going on? To subdue my fear, I turned and looked Fagu in the eyes. He stared back. The duel didn't last long. Someone from his gang came in with a bottle of wine, leaving the question as to who'd blink first unanswered. In that minute, I didn't care one way or the other. The two of them began to drink and made a lot of noise to attract attention. I got back to my meal, and Vilma and Lulu followed my example. While we were eating in silence, I realised that Fagu was back to his old tricks. The old mummy-daddy game. A bead of cold sweat broke out on my temples and dripped down the side of my face. My two companions were fortunately too absorbed in their meals, and the two men at the other table were probably too far away to notice a bead of sweat, if they were looking in my direction. "No need to show off like that," I thought, as I assessed Fagu's threatening gestures from the corner of my eye. "Don't think for one second that I'm afraid of you," I continued. All the time I had the impression that he could read my thoughts. "You're more of a bastard than I am, even though you don't have an uncle who's fled the country. I've been through more than you can imagine, you scumbag. Your childish games don't interest me any more than they did when we were little. You should at least have brains enough to understand that you'll only get Vilma, that gentle being of silk and satin, if you can see the tip of your unwashed ears without a mirror. There's no need to be afraid of me. I'm not your rival. Not because I'm afraid of you, but because there's no love left in me. I have a heart of ice. But you don't even understand that."

Vilma didn't come to work the next day. The day after

that, Lulu brought me a sealed envelope. She told me that
Vilma wanted to have my reaction verbally. She then withdrew to her corner of the laboratory and dissolved into the
lifeless objects around her. With the envelope in my hand,
and seeing Lulu's fragile figure receding into the corner, I
sensed danger. I'd heard of dozens of romances in our little
dust-covered town, and they all began with a letter. Nobody
could get enough of them. They started with a piece of
paper and who knows how they ended. For the young guys
in town, living in a century devoid of romance, there was
nothing more fascinating or important. The fortunate
recipients of such letters found naive ways of making sure
that everyone found out that they'd been received. Yet the
sending of that kind of letter involved certain rules which
were to be respected by all parties. Otherwise you could
end up with a knife in your stomach. When Lulu placed the
envelope with Vilma's letter in my hand, I could see the
blade of a knife. I could smell the man-eating tiger not far
off, and I stood back to catch my breath. Vilma was a
typical girl of the town. She too was living in a century
devoid of romance. I stuffed the letter into my pocket. I
didn't have the slightest interest in an erotic adventure. I
looked around at Lulu as she meditated over her test tubes.
I wanted to scream at her, "Go and tell Vilma that she's
acting like a brat and I haven't the slightest wish to deal
with her childish fantasies". Right then, Lulu looked over
towards me, and I felt sorry. Sorry for her and for Vilma.
Vilma wanted to entice me into a game. I knew that the
game would be half reality, half fiction. Maybe, more than
anything, I thought, it was her desire to escape into a dream
world. When they're sleeping, people aren't able, at least not
consciously, to distinguish between dreams and reality. The
letter was beautifully written, with bold, round strokes: "Do
you remember Max? Let's talk about Max. If you accept,
L. will tell you everything else." That was all. There was not
even an initial at the bottom. I was upset, angry in fact, but
it was pointless. I needed no further proof that Vilma was

still a child, naive and provincial. Once again, I didn't understand, as in the case of Sonia, that I'd made a serious mistake in my judgment of people.

I gave Lulu a sign and she arrived instantly like a remote-controlled robot, with clear and certain apprehension in her eyes, of course. She looked like a frightened dog that was used to being kicked around by its master. She studied my expression when I asked her what I ought to do. "I have to meet Vilma," I explained. "Tell me, how should I do it?" Lulu looked relieved. How her expression suddenly changed will always remain for me one of the great wonders of nature. A miracle. She took the letter and envelope from me and burned them with the flame of an alcohol lamp. "I'll be waiting for you at five o'clock at the edge of the garden," she said. "Follow me into the building. Don't be afraid. That's where I live – it's my apartment. Second floor. Vilma will be waiting for you there." Then Lulu withdrew to her corner of the laboratory and once again merged with the mass of lifeless objects.

On that day, I was busy with the analysis of dross and slag. I didn't know whether to laugh or cry. The prehistoric building of the plant moaned and quaked under my feet. Its guts rumbled like those of a poisoned stomach. As I was mounting the metal staircase of one of the silos, I had the impression, in the middle of the suffocating mixture of smoke and dust, that the end of the world was nigh. The feeling was so intense that I almost screamed. No one would've heard me anyway. Why had I exposed myself to Vilma's game?

It was a grey and yet scorchingly hot and humid afternoon. The sky was like a desert and the heat it poured on the town drenched everyone in sweat. I avoided the tavern which at that time of day was usually full to the brim. Right to the last minute, I hoped and prayed there'd be no Lulu at the edge of the garden. But it was not to be. She was there, right on time, discreet and attentive. "Lulu," I thought to myself, "I'm going to strangle you." She saw me coming and started to move. I followed her at a distance, shuffling along in my impotent gait. I felt impotent in all respects. That's what I wanted to tell Vilma right from the start, the second I got to Lulu's apartment. She had just gone in and left the door open behind her. Vilma was waiting in the living room, wearing a long dress and with her blonde hair flowing in cascades. Something was missing beside her. I thought for a minute. Yes, it was Lulu missing. "Lulu, you old procuress," I thought. "Your mistress sends you off as a message-bearer whenever she wants, does she?" Vilma was blushing. I sat down across from her, with a coffee table between us. Lulu wasn't there. Maybe for this reason neither of us could find the right words to begin. Lulu then came in with two cups of coffee and two glasses of juice, which she placed on the table between us and then she slipped away as discreetly as before. Vilma drank her juice, and then sipped at her coffee. I followed her example. First the juice, then the coffee. My wish to confess my impotence to Vilma had become a virtual obsession when suddenly the memory of Sonia loomed in front of me. She had come into the room and sat down beside Vilma as if to prove to me that my being alone with an innocent, blonde creature who I'd dreamt about so often, could only be an illusion, a trick, some sort of mirage. I was dying to know whether Vilma had ever slept with a man. And if so, how did she act during orgasm? Sonia, for example, howled. If the windows were open, you could hear her from quite a distance. Linda moaned. She always seemed to climax in great agony and suffering. I raised my eyes and stared at Vilma, giving her what might be regarded as a lascivious stare. She showed no sign of being uncomfortable, except that the glass in her hand shook a little. She placed the glass back on the coffee table so that I wouldn't notice. Vilma grinned and blushed once again. I arrived at the conclusion that she'd never slept with anyone. What appals me even today is that I can't even remember what we talked about.

I was delirious. I can recall only a few words. Max's name hovered in the air like a pesky piece of fluff. Occasionally, the old procuress Lulu would appear and vanish like some guardian angel. I can vaguely recall my impotence, my absent-mindedness, my heavy eyelids and hands, my parched brain. One thing I do remember clearly though. When I finally sneaked out of Lulu's apartment like a thief, I made a beeline for the tavern. And who did I run across there but Fagu and five or six of his companions! I ordered a glass of cognac and retreated to my table at the other end of the room. I could sense their piercing eyes fixed on me. I tried to concentrate and find out where the man-eating tiger was lurking. It was there. I could smell it like a dog. I took another large gulp. Coincidentally maybe, Fagu took a gulp of his cognac at the same time. Maybe coincidentally, too, our eyes met. "You can't be my tiger, you bastard, you're too busy tormenting Vilma. I was just with her. Your name wasn't even mentioned, though your spectre hovered above us in the room. She's never slept with anyone. She certainly won't with you, and that's never going to change. You probably want to ask how I know. The answer's simple. Vilma told me. You fool, do you think girls ever talk about it openly when they have sex with somebody? Don't stare at me like that with those droopy eyes of yours. You've terrified Vilma. You've terrified her to the point that she doesn't dare to go out with anyone because she knows that your thugs will lynch the guy on the spot. You haven't changed one bit. You're the same crazed, bloodthirsty, deceitful bastard you always were. Vilma brought up the subject of Max. You know very well that I was the one who killed him. You still torment anyone who gets too close to her, just like you did Sherif, the little gypsy boy who once teased her. She told me about that, too. She's disgusted at the very mention of your name. She met me in Lulu's apartment because she was afraid of you. Do you know what it means when a girl invites a boy out and arranges to meet him in a private apartment?"

Suddenly, Fagu stood up with a glass in his hand and sauntered towards me. His companions stayed in their seats and sluggishly watched what their boss was up to. I shifted my weight onto the other leg and took another sip of cognac. He loomed in front of me scowling, his face flushed with alcohol. Then he smiled, or rather smirked. I noticed that one of his upper right teeth was missing. He looked me over as if we were meeting me for the first time. "How about getting off that high horse of yours and coming over for a drink with the guys?" He swirled his cognac and fell silent for a minute. "I know you usually associate with a better class of people. We're nothing but flies to you. They say that mules forget the stable they were brought up in. That's the way you are. If we're only flies, you're nothing but a flea. So tell me, Mr. Student, what's better, flies or fleas? If you ask me, they're both the same. Don't put on airs. Keep to your own group. And most of all, prick up your ears, pay attention to where you're going! You can slip if you don't watch where you're going. And if you slip, you can easily break a leg, can't you?"

Fagu drank up his cognac. The glass had been full and his eyes suddenly welled with tears from the alcohol. The warning he'd given me couldn't have been more obvious. Vilma was out of bounds. He went back to his admirers. I stood leaning against my table with the glass in front of me. Fortunately, at that moment, Dori came into the tavern. He looked around, got himself a double from the bar, and came over to me. Dori drank down the whole glass, just as Fagu had done, but no tears welled in his eyes. I wanted to tell him that he was one of the rare people who showed no sign of fear at being stalked by the man-eating tiger, but he wouldn't have understood. He looked depressed. This became more obvious when he went back to the bar for a second double. He explained the reason to me later. He'd had a fight with his fiancée. After we'd drunk another glass together, I thought it was time for me to tell him the reason for my less than jovial mood: the fact that Fagu was threatening me. Dori advised me to be careful, adding with an ironic and bitter smile that it wouldn't be a bad thing, if the occasion arose, for me to get my nose up my girlfriend's knickers and thereby devastate Fagu and bring him down. I was now the one to give a bitter chuckle, firstly because Dori's words were to the point of being vulgar, and secondly, because I had no interest whatsoever in getting my nose up the knickers of my so-called 'girlfriend', as Dori'd referred to her. There was now a huge commotion on the other side of the room. A glass had been shattered. It looked as if a fistfight might be going to break out momentarily. But this wasn't the case. Just as he'd done a few days earlier in the canteen, Fagu'd deliberately dropped a glass to draw attention to himself. I realised this the moment I looked in his direction. "Poor fool," I thought to myself. "You'll have to break a whole warehouse of glasses to get the attention you need." I felt sorry for him, really sorry. He was suffering in his way, as I was in mine. In fact, we were all suffering in one way or another. Even Dori, who for some unknown reason had had a fight with his fiancée that evening, and after downing a fourth or fifth glass, asked me to walk him home.

# 14

Vilma had to have noticed my indifference, and she at least had enough sense to change what needed to be changed in her behaviour. This was obvious the day after our meeting at Lulu's apartment. She didn't repeat her invitation for us to have lunch together. Lulu didn't bring me any more letters, and when she looked in my direction, her eyes were scornful, though not hostile. At that time I was again obsessed by the idea of suicide. I spent my days and nights in deathlike monotony. But I couldn't bring myself to do the deed. I was simply too average, too ordinary. Even if they'd executed my father and interned me in some godforsaken village at the end of the earth, I'd still not have been man enough to commit suicide. Ladi was of a different calibre. He committed suicide. But before that became widely known, news of another event spread through town: the execution of my father.

Actually, the news that they'd blown the brains out of former comrade What's His Name at the edge of a ditch was received in town like a sports bulletin, but without the habitual commentaries. Most people couldn't have cared less. Eternally enveloped in clouds of dust and dogged by grey and often more sinister chronicles, the townspeople had immured themselves in a very realistic attitude to life. The man-eating tiger was there, stalking everyone. It was an age when no-one felt safe, neither the fortunate in their good fortune, nor the unfortunate in their misfortune. Neither the tormenters nor the tormented. Neither the clever nor the fools. Neither the righteous nor the sinners. They were all terrified of the tiger and were all afraid of each other. Because of this, the news of the execution of former comrade What's His Name could only be received and interpreted like a sports report, bare of commentary.

My father, who was always a cautious man, had advised me to keep out of sight for a while, and to restrict my movements to the road to and from work, not stopping anywhere else. It was a good piece of advice and I followed it. Until the day I received another bit of news: the suicide of Ladi.

It's one of the absurdities of my life that Ladi's suicide became the reason why I renewed my broken ties with Vilma. That is, if anyone could speak of a re-establishment of relations between us. It was the middle of October. We were having a few days of such splendid weather that it's hard to believe such a tragedy could have happened. But tragedy was in the air. My father informed me about Ladi's death in the most heartless way you could imagine. I'd just arrived home from work and was resting on the sofa in the kitchen, being forced to listen to the radio. I say being forced because my mother was a great fan of plays and had turned on the radio to listen to some epic love drama. My father, whose face by this time was showing signs of age, came into the room, sat down beside me and told me a friend had hanged himself. Those were his words: "That friend of yours has hanged himself". Mother, who was captivated by the plot of the drama, was concentrating on her radio programme. I was listening to it, too, and didn't understand the significance of the expression 'that friend'. Our lack of reaction caused father to provide more details. I heard from him that a man had hanged himself in his room and had been dangling there for five days before someone noticed he was missing and raised the alarm. "They say the body was already badly decomposed," sighed my father. "Poor lad." "What did he ever have out of life," wondered my mother, "with his father dead and his mother who knows where? He was a frail boy, with a face as pale as... a ghost, God forgive me for saying that." I sat up, startled by mother's words. She had an inquisitive nature and had no problem listening to two programmes at the same time, the epic love story on the radio and the news broadcast by my father. I'd like to have asked her which of the dramas she preferred. My parents were now staring at me. Father had gone pale and mother, with tears rolling down her cheeks, finally turned off the radio. I got up and locked myself in my room. Ladi's eyes with their ever-present sorrow were watching me. I imagined him in a noose, hanging from the ceiling or dangling from the iron bars of a window with his tongue sticking out and his eyes bulging. I wanted to throw up. A stench spread through the room and I had the impression I'd suffocate if I stayed inside. Everything was topsy-turvy: the walls, the ceiling, my desk, the bed, and everything stank. I went outside, but the stench of death was everywhere. Everything had died and was rotting.

I don't know exactly what got into me that made me head for Lulu's. In view of the circumstances, there were quite a few dangers involved. It was a warm afternoon with a lot of people in the streets, so it seemed likely that someone might see me going into her apartment building. It was possible, too, that Lulu would slam the door in my face and chase me away if she were startled by my sudden appearance or just because she had no particular reason to treat me with courtesy. Since my last visit to her apartment, our relations had been reduced to zero. Why would Vilma even want to come over and meet me at Lulu's apartment after being insulted by my indifference the last time? But I wasn't overly concerned about any of this right then. I had the impression that I was sinking into a marsh which was sucking me in, deeper and deeper, and that I needed something to hang on to, a branch or a blade of grass. Vilma's eyes appeared in front of me. If I couldn't find Vilma that afternoon, I felt I'd go crazy. Lulu certainly thought I was crazy. She cried out the moment she opened the door. I was shaken, so I looked over my shoulder, to the right and to the left. Fortunately, there was no one else in the stairwell behind me. This was decisive for Lulu's reaction. She scowled, and with open disdain, she stretched her hand out in my direction. At first I thought that she was going to shove me away and slam the door, but instead Lulu grabbed me and yanked me into the apartment with a force that I hadn't expected from such a fragile person. In any case, I was now in the apartment and the door was quickly shut behind me. She faced me, eyeing me with complete neutrality but was resolved not to let me take another step before explaining the reason for my visit. I didn't know what to say and stood there in silence, but the state I was in was explanation enough. My expression, my eyes, my whole condition must have spoken for me. Lulu led me into the kitchen. I sat down on the sofa, still not saying a word, and she started to make coffee. While we drank it, I managed to tell her that I'd come to see Vilma, that I had to meet her and would be really grateful if she could go and inform her. Lulu frowned, as if to say "Who does he think he is?" Then she went out. It seemed like ages before she got back. I was awakened by the sound of the key in the lock. Vilma was by herself, and came into the kitchen where I was still sitting. I was struck again by her blonde hair flowing in cascades, her azure eyes and gentle expression. Her eyes reminded me of Ladi's.

I had a lump in my throat when Vilma sat down beside me. "Ladi hanged himself," I stated in a matter-of-course way that sent a chill down my spine. Did she even know who I was talking about? She listened quietly and nodded. "I know," she responded. "I just heard. Everyone knows. Your friend hanged himself. I'm so sorry. I saw you once together on the boulevard. He looked like a nice guy and I'm so very sorry for you." I wanted to reply that her eyes were the same colour as Ladi's and maybe for this reason I had come to her. If I hadn't come, I wouldn't have known what to do with all the pain. I wanted to tell her how incredible it all seemed to me. But I said nothing. If I'd spoken, she would have heard the quiver in my voice, heard me break into a sob.

Lulu brought us some juice again and left us alone. I

don't remember what we talked about that day either, until I sneaked out in the evening. My brain wasn't working and I wasn't able to communicate properly, not even with Vilma. Our meeting the next day has been erased from my memory, too, just as if it was deleted from a tape. I can only remember having the impression that Vilma was hiding something from me and that there was something she wanted to tell me. The impression was so strong that on the third day I actually said to her: "You're hiding something". On our two previous meetings we had sat together all the time, but on the third day she stayed on the other side of the table, near the window, but not out of fear of me. Vilma had no reason to be afraid of being alone with me or of our physical proximity. The distance across the table was no chasm. The real abyss that I couldn't overcome and didn't want to overcome was inside me. Vilma stayed where she was because she was debating whether to say something to me, and this only reinforced the impression I had. When I accused her of hiding something, she turned her back on me. I sat on the sofa, bewildered, and stared at her cascading golden hair. She was a blonde Niagara. A Niagara Falls that you could plunge into and never reach the bottom. "My family came from the village of K," she retorted abruptly, still facing the window. "My father was born there, but I've never been there myself. I was born in this town. Father rarely went back, although he had relatives there and said it was a wonderful village. I used to beg him to take me to K with him to get to know the relatives. He'd invent all sorts of excuses not to go, until I discovered the real reason. My father did not want to take me back to his village because, as I learned from a cousin a few years ago, the village was full of internees. My father's village was an internment camp. Father knew what he was doing by not taking me."

Vilma fell silent. She still had her back to me and was looking out of the window. Was it possible that this angelic creature with the golden Niagara Falls hair that I could plunge into and never be seen again, was really Xhoda's daughter? He hadn't yet become Xhoda the Lunatic. He was only Xhoda the Terrible, guard dog over the childhood of generations of nobodies. Whenever our paths crossed, Xhoda would frown and pretend not to be watching me. His dislike of me first became pathological when I was expelled from university and my biographical time bomb became known. Xhoda the Terrible couldn't forgive me for having deceived him for years by not divulging this information which he considered was my duty to reveal to him. He didn't forgive me or my father and wouldn't greet either of us, not even look in our direction. It was as if, from the corner of our eyes, we were injecting him with some kind of disease – as if, if we'd attempted to greet him, he'd be bitten by a mad dog. Maybe we even looked like mad dogs to him and he was just trying to keep away from them. Vilma stayed silent and continued looking out the window with her back turned. It occurred to me that the guard dog of my childhood was possibly only striving to protect his daughter. Guard dog Xhoda knew very well what an internment village was. An internment village with all the goings-on of the internees wouldn't have been a suitable object for the eyes of a being like Vilma. She was too gentle a creature to see an internment camp filled with the faces of internees. I believed that Xhoda loved his daughter so much that he was capable of the craziest and most unimaginable acts, like mowing down half the men in town with a semi-automatic rifle. It was nothing unusual that Xhoda the guard dog should want to protect his daughter from anything or anyone who might have a negative influence on her well-being. If she'd glimpsed the faces of the internees, Vilma might have become ill.

"That cousin of mine is about the same age you are," said Vilma suddenly. "Her name is Tanci. Have you ever heard of a girl called Tanci?" she added, and turned quickly towards me. The cascade of hair changed direction. Golden Niagara began to flow behind her. Vilma put her hand to her forehead and then let her fingers slide down her face. "When father used to talk about Tanci, I always imagined her as a real ball of energy. I thought of her as a passionate dancer, frolicking with the mountain goats on the cliffs above her father's village. From my father's description, the village of K sounded like a quaint place for tourists. But the village and Tanci were nothing like I'd imagined them. I would maybe never have met Tanci, if she hadn't come to Tirana to meet me. Of course, she didn't come just to meet me. When we met, she told me that fate had finally smiled on her to let her see Tirana. She was a nice girl. She had coarse hands, rougher than those of the men working in the brigade you were in. She had a sturdy build, agile, but there was some physical deformity I can't really describe. Tanci was a clever girl. Three days with her were enough for me to understand how little I knew about life, or, to be honest, how spoiled and pampered I was."

Vilma left the window and came and sat down at the table, lessening the distance between us. I was still on the sofa leaning against the spongy backrest with my eyes downcast. I could feel the weight of Vilma's glance and looked up. She looked down at the floor, too. Maybe she could feel the weight of my glance now. I looked for Ladi's eyes in her expression. I had accused Vilma of hiding something from me and couldn't understand why she'd chosen that very day to tell me about her cousin with the odd name of Tanci. "Whenever I think about her," Vilma said, "I just want to cry. I wouldn't have mentioned her at all, if I hadn't bumped into her a couple of days ago. Tanci's getting married next week. She was in Tirana to do a bit of shopping and she's invited me to the wedding. But I'm not going. Father would never allow it anyway. But that's another story. Tanci told me something you might be interested in. She mentioned some woman…"

This was the third afternoon I'd spent with Vilma and when she started going on about some woman, I got fed up. I wanted to let her know that I wasn't interested in her stories about women. And I could imagine the woman she was talking about wasn't exactly Brigitte Bardot anyway. Tanci would never have spoken about Brigitte Bardot because BB hadn't made her appearance in Tanci's village yet. And even if she had, what interest would that be to me?

But it was of interest to Vilma. According to Tanci, the woman was an exceptional beauty, even if she wasn't called Brigitte Bardot. "Everyone who saw her when she arrived at the village, on the back of a truck, was overwhelmed. She's now living in K," added Vilma, "in a building which houses the internees." I also learned that everyone avoided Tanci's Brigitte Bardot. Tanci had learned that a certain vehicle would turn up every week at the foot of the mountain, right in front of the building where the internees were housed. At first, no one knew who or what the car was bringing, taking away and then bringing back again. It was an old Soviet Gaz, dark green, still in good condition, and with the curtains drawn in the back windows. It arrived every Tuesday at exactly ten in the morning, stayed for only a few minutes and then drove back in the opposite direction, leaving a cloud of dust behind it. It would come back the same evening or at night when the village at the foot of the mountain was lost in oblivion. People heard the noise of the motor and knew that the Gaz was making its way down the bumpy road leading to the building with the internees. The first detail to be uncovered was who was being picked up and returned the same evening. It was the strange, beautiful woman. No one in the village thought much of it at the start. It was nothing unusual for jeeps to be coming and going to take internees from the village into town and vice versa. It was well known who they were working for. Suspicions rose when it was found out that the beautiful woman wasn't being taken into town simply for interrogation purposes. It wasn't known who first stuck his nose into the situation or how he discovered the real purpose of the Gaz which turned up on such a regular basis. Maybe it wasn't one individual at all. The most likely version of events is that the enigmatic movements of the beautiful woman were uncovered by her admirers, the men who had been after her all the time. Their interference undid all the precautions taken. The strange, beautiful woman wasn't being driven into town after all. She was being taken through town into a forest and then to a nature reserve with a hunting lodge in it. There, the beautiful woman would meet someone – a person with grey eyes. In the hunting lodge she'd be alone in a room with a man with grey eyes and there were rumours in the village that she would make love to him. Others said she was involved in espionage.

I jumped up from the sofa, seized Vilma by the shoulders and held my body tight against hers. She looked pale, and fear troubled the calmness of her blue eyes. My ears were ringing all the time as she told me her story, or rather Tanci's, once again, including the noise of the old Soviet Gaz bumping its way down the road to the village in a cloud of dust. It wasn't carrying Brigitte Bardot, that was for sure. But maybe Brigitte Bardot screamed during orgasm like someone else, like Sonia. So vivid was the scream that echoed in my ears as Vilma told me about the nocturnal adventures of the beautiful woman in the lodge that I could see Sonia in the arms of Grey Eyes. Sonia was just as incapable of killing herself as I was. But now she was going through living death, in the form of Grey Eyes' breath on her body. "I just thought you might be interested," gasped Vilma, and her azure blue eyes still betrayed her fear. I was holding her by the shoulders, not sure whether I should throw her out the window or plunge into the azure of her eyes. I let her go and slumped back onto the sofa. Vilma was terribly upset. She stood there like someone who, by a stroke of luck, had escaped certain death from strangulation. I left Lulu's apartment. It was already getting dark.

# 15

The next day, I started my shift at the tavern. A curse was on me.

The tavern was empty. I remember that a twelve or thirteen-year-old boy came up and greeted me. He took an envelope from his back pocket and handed it to me. I grabbed it mechanically and, without the presence of mind to ask who it was from, stuffed it into my own back pocket. I almost told him that he was as beautiful as Hermes, the messenger of the gods. I'd once seen a drawing portraying him as a young boy with winged feet. I decided not to mention Hermes in case the boy might think I was crazy. Instead, I offered him a baklava, but he declined. Maybe he didn't eat baklava. On the other hand, maybe it was beneath his dignity to be invited by me. Giving me a less than friendly smile, Hermes from the riverside went out. I was tempted to have a look at the envelope, but instead I went over to the bar and ordered another cognac. I suspected who the envelope was from, what was in it and what it was about. The barmaid, an old friend from my school days, taking advantage of the fact that the tavern was empty, begged me not to drink anymore. I thanked her. She didn't know that a curse was on me, otherwise she wouldn't have given me such a useless piece of advice. And, what was the big deal about anyway? Why shouldn't I drink? I was so insignificant that my drinking could in no way jeopardise public morals, not to mention the fact that no one had yet been able to measure and exactly determine how many millilitres of alcohol and how many centimetres a skirt could be above the knee so as to be enough to shake the foundations of public morals. I wasn't supposed to drink and women weren't supposed to wear miniskirts. The government permitted alcohol to be sold, but it didn't allow miniskirts. So it wasn't me, but the government that was responsible for my drinking. The government was also responsible for the fact that women weren't in miniskirts. This was more or less the line of reasoning on which I expounded to the barmaid. She broke up, laughing so much that she offered me a free double cognac. "Don't think that you can get the best of me with your jackass jokes," she said as I returned to my corner of the tavern. "I only gave you the cognac because you are a good guy and will go home like a gentle little lamb as soon as you drink up."

I waved at her and took a sip. Then another. I wouldn't be getting another drink out of my old classmate from school, that was for sure. What I needed was to calm down, reflect and find my balance in the world, because the curse was on me. And in order to find my balance, I had to use logic and pure philosophical reasoning. And to attain this logic and philosophical reasoning, I had to keep drinking until my objective, the restoration of my balance, equated with the emptiness of the glass. I reasoned, as I took little nips of cognac, that this had all happened because neither Sonia nor I are the type of people to have the courage to kill themselves when the moment comes. Neither Sonia nor I belong to that category of individuals who find solutions to overcome all impediments. Sonia must have thought the same thing, I argued. Nothing else mattered. Nothing else mattered at all. Grey Eyes expedited the old, but well-kept Soviet Gaz several times, and finally, Sonia gave in and applied logic. Of course, Grey Eyes' deal with Sonia wasn't easy to achieve. On the other hand, Sonia's deal with him wasn't easy either. An agreement could only be reached by negotiation. Sonia sold what she had to offer. But what price did Grey Eyes pay? That wasn't important either. In the end, Sonia submitted to logic and made a deal. The Gaz picked her up and took her into town, or at least that's what the morons thought. The vehicle actually continued its trip through town and through the large pinewood forest to the nature reserve with the hunting lodge at Grey Eyes' disposal. Nothing else mattered. A deal was done. Sonia at least had the right to make a deal.

The last drop of cognac was drunk. I felt like a fish out of water, parched and thirsty for another drink. From the corner of my eye, I looked desperately at the barmaid, knowing she wouldn't give me any more to drink. She was a good-natured old girl, but no matter what I might do to entice her, she wasn't going to give me another glass. But there was nothing humming in her ears. The noise in my ears was a roar. Her ears couldn't hear the engine of the old Soviet Gaz as it rumbled through the forest. And they couldn't hear Sonia's footsteps on the parquet floor of the lodge. My ears heard it all. "Hey, old girl, gimme something to drink, will you," I wanted to holler. "I can't stand Sonia's screams and Grey Eyes' panting. They're driving me crazy. The creaking of the old wooden bed to the rhythm of their naked, intertwined bodies is driving me insane!" I would have torn the barmaid to shreds right then, if a second person hadn't come into the tavern. It was no messenger of the gods this time, but my guardian angel, Dori.

According to Dori, I was in an aggressive mood that morning. I don't understand why Dori gave me the same piece of advice as the barmaid – he told me to stop drinking. It was beyond imagination. When I asked Dori if he had a letter for me, too, he seized me by the arm and dragged me out of the tavern almost by force. He probably thought I was making fun of him or I was so drunk that I didn't know what I was saying. But I wasn't making fun of him and I still knew what I was saying. I protested that the means by which he'd chosen to drag me out of the tavern constituted violence. "And I shall protest against the use of violence. The only people allowed to use violence," I continued, "are Grey Eyes and the representatives of the Dictatorship of the Proletariat. The Dictatorship of the Proletariat is the imposition of the truth by means of violence. It is now imposing violence in an exemplary manner in an oak wood bed in a hunting lodge made of pine, although it is here more a question of pure rape than of simple violence…"

A slap in the face brought my rant to an end. We were standing inside the park in the middle of town. Surrounded by privet hedges, I gave Dori a reproachful glance. He laughed scornfully. "If you really want to end up in jail, just keep on raving," he said. "I certainly don't intend to go along with you. If you say one more word, I'm going to punch you." It was my turn to snicker this time. "What a coward and a bastard you are!" I retorted, but in a lower voice. I'd become as quiet as a clam. "Can't you at least own up? I admit I'm a clam." I was then on the point of adding a few philosophical observations with regard to clams – a government of clams, the Dictatorship of the Clams, but didn't have the energy. A lump stuck in my throat and I vomited on the spot at the edge of the garden, throwing up on all the privet hedges powdered in cement dust. Then Dori took me home. When we got there, I made a speech on the universal character of clam governance. Dori listened to my spouting as he was drinking the coffee mother had made for him. Then he took off and I fell asleep. The only thing I remembered was Dori's urgent request for me to meet him the next day as soon as I got up. I wasn't at all interested in why I should meet him, so I stood snickering at the head of the stairs, slumped against the banister, and waved, yelling: "Farewell, my good clam".

Farewell my good clam! Farewell! But where? Why? My brain was buzzing with questions as soon as I opened my eyes as if I'd spent the whole night fixating on why Dori wanted to meet me. The day looked like a void, like the empty shell of a clam. An inauspicious day with all the signs of doom. Not only because a black cat crossed my path as I went down the front stairs. I'm actually not sure about the colour of the cat. It might have been grey. Whatever, it was a cat, grey or black, and not a tiger. It was a simple member of the carnivorous feline race, one of its most benign representatives, though this may be the reason why it was reputed to bring bad luck. At the edge of the privet-enclosed park, on the street leading down to the tavern door, sat a large fellow with a frown on his face and his arms folded over his chest. There was anger in his expression, and the moment I saw him, I realised that doom was upon me. It was Xhoda. I had the distinct impression that he'd left his house and had taken up position there just for me. At first I wanted to cross the street, as you would if a black cat crossed your path. But since I have no interest in cats, grey or black, I continued down the road and walked right by him without so much as a nod or greeting. I was intent on getting to the tavern as quickly as possible to find solace in a large glass of cognac, a whole bottle if possible, so as not to make a scene by screaming or shouting the most vulgar expressions the universe had ever heard. But Xhoda had plans of his own. He was not one to go out and plant himself somewhere like a stake in a garden fence to keep an eye on pedestrians. He snorted as I walked by. I almost didn't realise that he had something to tell me. The guard dog of my childhood was actually paying me the honour of lying in wait for me in broad daylight at the entrance to the tavern, the most appropriate venue for an ambush. In a normal ambush, there is always a hail of machine-gun fire or at least a grenade hurled. Xhoda's grenade was the warning: "You are going to have to prick up your ears, boy," and then he spat at me. I retorted that my ears were fine the way they were. It was a superfluous remark, but at least it was an answer. How could I have guessed the reaction this remark would have on Xhoda. He turned red in the face, and his huge body, a head taller than I was, shuddered. "You bastard," he shouted, "you're gonna bite the dust!" He repeated this several times, but more for himself. I'd turned my back to him and left him standing on the sidewalk beside the privet hedges of the park. "You're gonna bite the dust, you're gonna bite the dust." It then occurred to me why Xhoda was so furious. I'd been with Vilma at Lulu's apartment for three days in a row. Three days in a row. And Vilma was Xhoda's daughter. Xhoda loved his daughter madly. Someone must have seen us or discovered that we were in Lulu's apartment together and informed Xhoda. A cold shiver ran down my spine. Not of fear, because I didn't even know what torment Xhoda reserved for anyone harassing his daughter, and I didn't belong to that category of individuals anyway. Yet my reply was a mistake and his reaction portended evil. I couldn't help but turn around and have a last look at Xhoda. He was standing on the same spot on the sidewalk and his furious expression was hurling bolts of lightning in my direction. There was no doubt about it. Someone had seen us.

I didn't go back to the tavern because I would have been stuck there all day. I headed for the plant. The smoke from the chimney stacks was rising vertically like a black column. It reminded me of the old caravan expression: 'Let the dogs bark and the smoke rise straight'. Or should it be 'Let the dogs bark and may the caravan be off'. "Let's not get tangled up here," I thought to myself. "Who are these dogs and what is the caravan anyway?" I stood slightly dazed for a while in front of the plant, and stared at the perfectly perpendicular column of black smoke rising undisturbed into the sky. If there had been the slightest breeze, or if the heavens had barked, the smoke would have spread confusion and consternation, and the caravan would have been destroyed. The balance of the cosmos would have been tipped. And I'd be biting the dust. Xhoda would force me to bite the dust, just as Ladi had. Sonia didn't like the taste of dust so she'd made a deal for herself. But what kind of deal could I make, and with who? Then I remembered that I had a meeting with Dori who'd pleaded with me not to forget it.

I couldn't find Dori. There was no one around the plant at all. Everything looked abandoned that day. Even the laboratory was empty. No Vilma, no Lulu to be seen. The void of it all frightened me. The roar of the mills sounded like a groaning from the bowels of the earth. "Is there anyone here?" I called out with all the force I could muster. There was no answer. The mills continued to turn. "Is there anyone here?" I repeated in despair. Then at one end of the laboratory I caught sight of a bonnet. It was covering the head of one of the laboratory assistants of the second shift, a woman in her fifties with a bloated, puffy face and a weary look. Whether from the deafening noise, from the bonnet she was wearing or from an excess of wax in her ears, she didn't hear my call. When she finally turned around and caught sight of me in the lab, she screamed. "No, I'm not the devil incarnate, you silly goose," I shouted back, knowing perfectly well that she couldn't hear me. She told me that Dori was at a meeting and that Vilma and Lulu hadn't come to work. She also informed me that she and another lab assistant who was out at the silos, had been called in urgently because no one else had shown up for the first shift. Where Vilma was, she didn't know, but Lulu was in hospital. When I asked why, she looked at me apprehensively. "She got beaten up," she explained, "really badly injured. She was coming home last night, when some guys attacked her in the dark and hit her over the head with something."

The swollen face of the laboratory assistant turned pale. I left. I'd heard enough. A shiver ran down my spine as it occurred to me that there was a connection between everything: Dori's urgent wish to talk to me, Xhoda's ambush, Vilma's absence and the attack on Lulu. I made my way straight to the hospital.

Lulu was in a room with four other recently-operated-on women. Fortunately, I knew the head of the surgery ward, who lived in my apartment building. He found a white gown for me and took me to the door of the room where Lulu was lying, asking me not to stay long. I felt nauseous as soon as I entered the room. At the far end there were two girls sitting on the bed of a woman who was moaning and groaning, begging for water, but neither of them gave any to her. The girls looked around at me as I came in and then turned their heads towards the bed on their right in which I suspected Lulu was lying. I froze. The willingness of the senior physician to let me into the ward was more kindness than I'd expected of a neighbour. Now the suggestive eyes of the girls were pointing me in the direction of the bed. There was no doubt in my mind that the whole town had already learned of my arrival in the ward and knew who I was visiting. I turned my back on the girls. The pungent smell of medication and heavy female transpirations made my stomach turn. I touched Lulu's forehead with the tips of my fingers. She recognized me and actually smiled. She'd been terribly battered. And yet she managed to give me a smile. Her face was green and blue and one eye was swollen. I took her hand which was dangling over the side of the bed and held it in mine. Then I bent over and pressed my lips against its soft skin and kissed it. After a moment of silence, I managed to murmur something like: "Lulu, who did all this to you? Tell me."

Lulu did her best once again to smile, which under normal circumstances she rarely did. But whenever she did smile, it was like a wonder of nature on her face. On that particular day, however, all you could see were bruises, swollen flesh and a glitter emanating from one eye. "It was dark," she stuttered. "They threw a sack over my head and started to beat me. Out of sheer spite I made no noise whatsoever, and said nothing. The more they beat me, the harder I clenched my teeth. When they'd had their fill, they left me lying in the apartment stairwell with the sack still over my head. Either they had beaten me enough or they were simply afraid of being seen. Two neighbours found me lying there like a sack of potatoes. The thugs were gone. At first, I didn't know what they wanted from me. I thought they were criminals and thieves trying to rob me. They certainly were criminals, but they were no thieves.

They resembled those guys you hang out with at the
tavern. Now I know why they did it. You understand, too,
don't you? So be very careful."

I stood there, holding her hand. "You're right," I
murmured. "What filthy bastards, beating up a woman and
then, only in a group. They only show their teeth in a pack,
like wolves." Lulu squeezed my hand as if to remind me
not to raise my voice. "Lulu," I said, "they've done this to
you because of me. From this second on, anyone who
comes near you will have to deal with me. Do you understand? If they so much as dare to touch a strand of your
hair, they'll have to deal with me." I felt her feebly squeez-
ing my hand again. I was sputtering nonsense, but I knew
I was ready to do anything I could to take revenge on them.

It was almost noon when I left the hospital. I avoided the
road past the tavern and instead, used a roundabout way to
get home, approaching the apartment building from
behind and sneaking into it like a thief. My unusual behaviour simply helped to reinforce the decision I'd taken while
with Lulu.

I couldn't forget the bruises on her face and her one
open eye. Her painful attempt to smile distressed me.
"Poor Lulu," I murmured, "why did they do it to you?" as
I turned the key in the lock. The apartment was empty.
Both mother and father were at work. The silence in the
rooms calmed my nerves and helped clear my cluttered
brain until I had the impression I could make a rational
decision. First, I brewed some coffee. As the pot was
coming to a boil, I saw them all drinking in the tavern. But
I wasn't interested in them all. I was only interested in one
of them, and that was Fagu. No one else.

The pot boiled over, spilling onto the stove, and the
room filled with the smell of burnt coffee. "What should I
do?" I thought to myself as I poured myself a steaming
cup. "Did you really think I'd sit back and put up with
everything? Most likely you did – in fact I'm sure you did.

135

'He's chicken,' you probably said to yourself, 'just some jackass student. He's not going to take risks for someone like Lulu. We'll kill two birds with one stone,' you thought. 'We'll teach that old procuress Lulu a lesson she'll never forget.'" Of course, there would be a huge uproar in town. People would find out why Lulu was beaten to a pulp with a sack over her head. Xhoda would find out, too. The first thing he'd do would be to sharpen his knife and put his daughter on a short line. Bravo, everything would go according to plan, up to that point. As Lulu told me later, Xhoda was in a rage and blew up at Vilma. He wouldn't let her leave the house, not even to visit her friend in the hospital. Everything according to plan. But there was no plan anyway. "There are so many ways you could have put the fear of god into Lulu and let Xhoda know what his daughter was up to. Why did you have to beat her up? Why did you and those two thugs of yours beat up some defenceless individual in the dark, a poor innocent girl who'd never harmed a fly? And batter her so badly that even you, Fagu, would be disgusted at yourself if you saw her. Some base instinct welled up in you, did it, Fagu? All you have are base instincts. I feel sorry for you, for you and your thugs. In fact, I feel sorry for us all. Let me ask you, what's happened to us? Do you have an answer? You smirk and guffaw, and think I'm the fool. The question doesn't even penetrate your sluggish brain. As for me, it tortures and terrifies me to see what's become of us. It horrifies me to think that my question will do no more than infuriate you, and provoke you to punch me in the nose – or worse. Go ahead and lose your temper, Fagu. If I remember correctly, your father was an officer when we were children. I don't know if he's still in the army or retired. He was a friend of Xhoda's and yet, Xhoda didn't beat you any less than he did me. My father let Xhoda beat me. Did your father acquiesce, too? Look at you, you're losing your temper. Don't take it so personally. We were caned our whole childhood long and we're still getting caned. That's what's wrong, Fagu. The cane leaves marks that not even the grave can erase. That's why violence against the weak is a matter-of-course thing for you and your thugs. Pretty nasty, you must admit, Fagu, isn't it? To beat up an innocent and defenceless girl like Lulu is pretty ugly, don't you think? Why the temper tantrum? I'm the one who should be angry. But as you can see, I am keeping my calm as I talk to you. Yet, I don't know if I'll be able to control my temper when we actually come face to face. And the moment will come, there's no doubt about it. Let's be honest, Fagu. You beat up poor Lulu to get at me. I got your message. But you made one small mistake. You forgot that I was born and raised in this town, too, and just like you, I was nourished on the dust and cement of these streets. We've both eaten dust and cement, Fagu, and have both learned to settle accounts in our own way. You're mistaken if you think you can intimidate me and force me to give up Vilma by beating up Lulu. You want Vilma, I know. It gives me the shivers to think that you're still playing the old games of our childhood. You're pathetic. If you'd had the courage to look me in the eyes and tell me man to man what your problem was, we could have avoided all this business for the simple reason that I'm not interested in Vilma. This is what makes your behaviour so tragic and absurd."

As I came out of my imagined soliloquy, I put my cup back on the table. The coffee had calmed my nerves and cleared my head. Yet there was something gnawing deep in my chest. I had the impression that a crab was lodged in my rib cage, and that if it moved, the cage would burst. It was my inner rage. Hunched up inside, but not pinching hard yet, it was waiting to see what I would do. I got up and went over to the clothes closet. There I found what I was looking for inside a small box stored under a disorderly heap of clothes: a knife. At work, I'd once come very close to using it against the optimists. It was a handsome weapon with a fine steel blade. I'd wrapped it in an oiled rag in a plastic bag kept in the wooden box. I wiped it off slowly and then polished it until it gleamed. With the knife in my hand, I lay down on the bed. I was breathing slowly and my heart was beating regularly. But a voice inside me told me to wrap the knife in the rag again, to put the rag in the plastic bag, to stick the plastic bag back into the box, to stuff the box back under the bundle of dirty laundry, and then go to bed. I wasn't sure if I was hearing the voice of my conscience or Vilma's voice. Maybe it was my voice talking to hers. In any case, I could hear Vilma. She was whispering to me in a low, agonizing tone as I stared at the blade. The problem was that I couldn't get to sleep. I didn't feel anything, no emotion. Vilma's voice wafted in from a distance, as if from another planet, although geographically speaking, she was quite near, locked in a house on the other side of the road a few hundred metres away. "Leave me alone," I whispered in a weary daze. "I want nothing to do with you. You're far too naive to get mixed up in all this business."

I went out, still in the company of Vilma's whispers. I wasn't sure what I felt for her, and didn't know what to call it. It was afternoon and the heat was sultry and oppressive. A dirty sky hung low over the town and for the first time in my life I wondered if the sky was really dirty or if it only seemed that way to me. Did it look dirty to Vilma when she gazed out the window of the room she was locked in? After all, I said to myself, why should Vilma and I see the world as being the same? There was no reason to assume that all people had an identical perception of things. Was red always red to everyone, and black always black? If you closed your eyes, the universe melted away, like when you're asleep. And sleep was only a step before death. Every twenty-four hours people trained for death. My hand instinctively felt for the place where I kept the knife, on the inside of the right leg of my trousers.

By that time of day, Fagu and his clan had usually staked their claim to the table in the opposite corner of the tavern to where I normally sat. My arrival was met with complete indifference. No one turned to look. This led me to believe that they were expecting me. I gave them a fleeting glance, trying to figure out which ones of them had attacked Lulu, and I then went over to the bar. The reaction of my school friend, the plump barmaid, confirmed the impression I'd had when coming into the tavern. She, too, sensed that the clan was waiting and on the prowl that day. "Be careful," she murmured, as she handed me a double cognac. "I suspect they're in a bad mood today." "So am I!" I retorted. "There's just something under my skin." The guys at the other end were sizing us up from the corners of their eyes. I'd pronounced the words "there's just something under my skin" loudly enough for them to hear. The barmaid looked scared and disappeared somewhere behind the counter. I grabbed my glass and sauntered over to my table at the end of the room. I sat down, leaned my elbow on the table and realised that they'd completely understood the special significance of my grey linen trousers. On the lower legs, the trousers had vertical zips covering pockets under the material, a style which a lot of people in town were wearing at the time. What was inside the pocket was obvious. At least the guys at the other table were well aware that my pocket wasn't either fake or empty. I'd put the trousers on when I got back from the hospital, knowing that I'd find Fagu and his clan here together, as usual. Nobody made a move. I noticed that none of them had trousers with vertical zips. But that didn't mean that their other pockets were empty.

A few minutes passed. I was beginning to think that nothing would happen that day, not only because none of them had zips on the pockets of their trouser legs. They seemed to be on their best behaviour. They were being so good that you'd almost have thought they were competing for a good conduct award. Fagu raised his head and gave me a furtive glance. There was something inscrutable in his eyes. "What's going on?" I thought to myself. "There's

something fishy about this good behaviour of yours."
Outside, on the other side of the road, I noticed a man
hanging around near the privet hedges of the park. He was
short, one of those people whose age you can never really
guess. His name was Llambro and he was reputed to be an
informant. There was nothing too unusual in the fact that
Llambro was standing out on the street, as he often did.
And there wasn't anything odd in the fact that, soon afterwards, a policeman came up and talked to him. What did
surprise me was that Fagu was constantly staring at them.
Most guys in town, with or without leg zips, avoided
informants and the police like the plague. What was Fagu
up to that day? I had another sip of cognac. His clan was
gathered around him, drinking. But not Fagu himself. He
was sitting in front of an empty tumbler, exchanging
glances with Llambro. "Bastard," I thought. "What are you
up to?" I put my glass back on the table. Suddenly I understood what was going on! Slowly, so as not to raise any
suspicion, I strolled over to the side of the bar where the
washrooms were. Instead of going in, I ducked behind the
counter and made a very low whistling noise. My plump
barmaid friend heard it and noticed me. I pressed my
index finger on my lips and called her over. Undoing the
zip, I removed the knife from my trouser pocket and
handed it to her, with my finger still on my lips. "Hide this,
will you?" I whispered. "Give it to me later. If I don't come
back for it, throw it away. Do whatever you want with it,
but don't give it to anyone else."

The barmaid did as I asked, and I went back to my
table. The pack was still drinking and Fagu kept staring out
the window. I had enough time to finish my cognac and
order another one. "For God's sake, don't drink so much,"
pleaded the petrified barmaid. "Don't worry, I'm not going
to drink any more," I responded, to calm her down. "But
just let me have a hunk of candy cane, will you?" Giving
me a curious stare, she wrapped the sweet in a bit of newspaper and put it on the counter. As I was going back to my

table, I noticed there were now two policemen talking to Llambro. After that, everything went quickly. Fagu got up and left his pack, heading in my direction. He kept one hand hidden behind his back. "You ass," I thought to myself. I was quick to throw my glass of cognac in his face before he could do the same to me. The tumbler in his hand plummeted to the floor. There was a cry. He seized the table and hurled it at me, trying to crush me against the wall. I leapt out of the way and the table crashed against the front window of the tavern. The barmaid screamed. The customers in the bar scattered. We wrestled and slugged one another in bitter silence. None of his clan intervened. Just as I'd suspected, the two policemen appeared on the scene almost immediately and separated us, one holding back Fagu and the other me. With them came an official in civilian clothing, known to everyone in town. Llambro had disappeared. Fagu and I surrendered without protest and were led off to the police station, both of us under the watchful eyes of curious bystanders.

The police station was a two-storey building just outside the centre of town. The moment I went in, I was subjected to a detailed body search. I emptied my pockets, with the exception of the zipped pocket in my right trouser leg, leaving the pleasure of uncovering illicit objects to the fellow responsible for making an inventory of my possessions. This was an officer with a huge, ruddy face and paws to match, who'd frighten the wits out of you. "What have we got here?" he asked with obvious delight in his voice, as if he'd finally caught me. "Don't you realise we know all about these tricks of yours?" Up to then, his behaviour had been exemplary. He'd given proof of admirable patience in face of the awkward and sluggish way I'd emptied my pockets, spilling earth-shattering objects such as bus tickets and coins, onto the table. He radiated, almost sincerely, as if to say: "Keep it coming. I can wait." There was a gleam in his eyes just like in those of a cat playing with a mouse. "Aha!" he triumphed, with his claws outstretched towards the zip of my right leg. "Why so nervous?" In a swift move, he ripped open the zip, stuffed his hand into my pocket and took out the piece of candy cane wrapped in paper. He held it up like a trophy, shifting it from one hand to the other, and unwrapped it slowly and carefully. A scrumptious sweet. "What is this all about?" he muttered, looking at the policeman standing next to me. "What is it?" I explained to him that it was a piece of candy cane and that, if he wished to, he was free to give it to his daughter at home. He rose from his chair in visible wrath (it was only later I discovered that he actually did have a daughter in secondary school). I felt a punch in the stomach and a kick in the shins, both at the same time, and sank to the floor in a cry of pain. There I got another kick in the ribs. These were the last items in the inventory of my belongings. Muscle-bound arms lifted me up and dragged me down the corridor. A door opened, I was hurled somewhere and the door was slammed behind me. I lay there with my face to the floor.

I don't how long it was before I dared to move. I was in agony from head to toe. After a while, I started to regain my senses and managed to pick myself up and get my body onto a bench next to the wall. There was no window in the cell. It was dimly lit by a single light bulb fixed to the ceiling. I could hear steps in the corridor from time to time. It almost made me laugh to think about the idiotic officer and his ruddy face who'd succeeded in confiscating my piece of candy cane. "I'll survive if I just keep my spirits up," I thought. As if to challenge my optimism, steps resounded once again in the corridor, steps which were getting closer and closer. Maybe they're bringing in Fagu for interrogation with me to clarify the incident, I mused. I hadn't seen him since we'd arrived at the police station. But it wasn't Fagu. The door creaked open and two tall police officers appeared, young cops who'd never seen in town, and would likely never see again. The door was shut and one of them came over to me, while the other stayed in the doorway. I was slumped on the bench, dying of thirst, and wanted to ask for some water. The one cop looked me over. "So where is the knife?" he demanded. "Where did you hide it? We know you had a knife. If we hadn't intervened, you would have committed a serious crime. Come on, out with it! What did you do with the weapon?" He didn't wait for an answer, but punched me in the stomach and kicked me in the shins, the same procedure I'd experienced earlier from the ruddy-faced officer. The effect was more or less the same. I gave a piercing scream and would have collapsed to the floor, if the cop hadn't grabbed me and held me back on the bench. The whole room spun around me. The light bulb above my head became a galaxy of revolving stars. In it I could see the face of the cop, severed from the rest of his body. Just a few strands of black hair falling over his forehead. As my vision gradually returned to normal, I could see pock-marks on his skin. I noticed the other cop approaching from the doorway. He shoved the first fellow with the pock-marked face aside and loomed in front of me. "Hey, you know what?" he said to his colleague with a smirk, "now I know where I've seen this guy before. I thought at first that he was the pickpocket we nabbed on the bus out to the plant a few days ago. He looks like him, but it's not the same guy. This one here looks like more of a pervert. In fact, if I hadn't seen him in the cell this morning, I'd have thought he was that son of a bitch who raped the fourteen-year-old girl two days ago near the abattoir. But now I know who he is. This snout-face reminds me of someone who was swaggering around the streets of Tirana a while ago, strutting from one bar to the next, as if he owned the town. This shit-face forgot who he was and where he came from. You should have known better, you rat!" he snarled, seizing me by the arms, "You should have known we'd catch up with you one day or another, you scumbag!"

I don't remember ever having met the person and

didn't understand how it was possible for him to hate me
so intensely without any reason. If my time had come, I
thought, better to die right away. I spat in his face. There
was fury in his eyes. I remember two punches in the nose
and one in the stomach. In my semi-conscious state, or
rather in the realm halfway between life and death, I recall
seeing myself in the bar of the Hotel Dajti. A drowsy
melody, something from the blues, echoed in my ears. In
the subdued lighting I could see Sonia and smell her hair
as I held her in my arms. There, at a round table in a
corner, sat Grey Eyes, watching us, and beside him was a
guy with a long-drawn-out, mongoloid face and prominent
cheeks. He had a policeman's cap pulled over his brow so
as not to be recognised. But I got a look at him. "Yes, it is
him," I thought, as I came to my senses.

They were gone. They must have left the room while I
was coming to, because I had the vague impression of
having heard voices and some obscene cursing. In any
case, there was no one else in the room and I found myself
staring up at the dim light bulb which was glowing from
the ceiling. My whole body was in tremendous pain and
my face was burning. It must have been terribly swollen,
probably black and blue. It felt more like someone else's
face or like a mask that had been made and rivetted to my
own face. I managed to prop myself up and get back on the
bench. There was no question about it – I was in serious
trouble. It was obvious that the whole thing had been a
trap. They'd done their best to catch me in possession of a
weapon, to put me away for months. That was clear. But
the beating I'd been given wasn't standard practice for the
municipal police. The ones who roughed me up weren't
police officers. Why would a couple of guys I'd never seen
be after me instead of the municipal police, uniformed or
not? The answer to this question would soon be provided.

I didn't even recognise him at first. Maybe because we
hadn't seen one another for a long time and he'd changed
in appearance. Maybe it was because I couldn't imagine

there might be a connection between my precarious situation and his arrival on the scene. It could also be simply that I didn't know who he was because I was in a terrible state and the lighting in the room was bad, so bad that his face seemed shrouded in mist. Yes, he appeared out of the mist. I was sitting on the bench, leaning back with my head slumped against the wall, too. I suddenly recognised him. I can't say that I had any particular reaction. I imagined that he'd come to use me as a punching bag, just like the two cops before him had done. "And so we meet again. You should have known we'd catch up with you sooner or later," he sneered. I didn't reply. What could I have said? I'd been snared. I was now prisoner of the Minister's son, the police investigator A.P. I was at the mercy of Grey Eyes. But then I changed my mind. There was something I wanted to say to him after all. I told him that I'd just heard the expression: "You should have known we'd catch up with you sooner or later," used by that colleague of his with the mongoloid face and prominent cheeks. "I imagine you remember that evening in the bar of the Hotel Dajti, don't you?" I asked to provoke him. "Your mongoloid friend was sitting next to you, but he was in civilian dress, not in a police uniform like he is today." Grey Eyes smiled again, or rather gave an unpleasant grin. He crossed his arms on his chest, looked me over, as his sidekick had done, and shook his head. "It doesn't look like you have learned your lesson," he noted. "We are going to have to continue teaching. But I haven't come for that."

He paused, unsure as to whether he should continue or not. I had time to get a good look at him and for a second I was struck by the thought that his thin, bloodsucking lips had been sucking at Sonja's, and that his tongue had been licking her nipples. Did he know that there would be no greater torture for me than to witness his leechlike lips on her body? I'd rather be beaten to a pulp and have my head knocked against the wall than to see those leeches sucking her blood out. "Not a bad job!" he remarked, as the leeches quivered. "You can't get caught red-handed if you're carrying a piece of candy cane instead of a knife. Congratulations. You were always a clever one. But were you clever enough? That is what I've come to find out. There is a certain Xhoda in this little town of yours, and that certain Xhoda has a certain good-looking daughter. They say he makes mincemeat of anyone who harasses her. But that's not the way you work. You don't harass girls, you devour them. The problem is that you sooner or later get devoured yourself. You thought you could fool everyone. But this isn't really why I have come. In fact, I might even be able to help you. You know, there is no sense in all this rivalry and hostility between us. I hated you and you hated me, and don't try to deny it. The question is, why? And the answer to that is: for no reason at all." He came closer and stared at me with his grey eyes. "That girl is not worth it. I originally thought she was something special, but now that I've had her, I see she's nothing to write home about. It's not just the fact she's got bad breath. I don't know how you managed to put up with that for so long. You must have a good stomach. I satisfied my curiosity and I've had enough of her. But as for you, my randy friend, well, curiosity is a funny thing. I've heard she's now having it with the village idiot, some guy who's retarded and slobbers all the time. It's pretty obvious she doesn't have much class. She's just a hysterical nobody."

Outside in the corridor, I could hear footsteps. Sometimes they'd stop as if someone might be putting his ear to the door and listening in. The footsteps would recede and then the whole process would begin again. Grey Eyes was covering his back. There was someone waiting outside in case he needed help. But I was in no position to resist, and it would have been a waste to spit on a guy like that. He was a walking ball of pus. What good would a bit of spit do on him? I gave a slight smile at first, and then a chuckle. The door opened and someone stuck his head in. With a wave of his hand, Grey Eyes told the intruder to get lost.

He said I should quit acting like a fool and stop playing games. "I've come to talk about something serious, something that might be of interest to you... It could be of interest to someone else, too. And by the way, I was only pulling your leg with the stuff about the village idiot."

The leeches contorted. Then they straightened out and slithered on top of each other. I had the impression that thousands of leeches were swarming all over my body, blotting out every centimetre of my skin and frenetically sucking my blood out. "Just so there is no misunderstanding," continued Grey Eyes, "your chances here are not good. You think you fooled everyone by hiding that knife you carry with you. I agree. I think you made idiots of them all, but they have a different opinion. There are people who are willing to testify that you had a knife in your trouser leg pocket while you were grappling with that guy. They apparently saw it and touched it."

I didn't know what he was getting at. An instinctive reflex told me to defend myself and contradict him. I declared that I'd never had a knife at all. This time it was his turn to smile. He became chummy all of a sudden and went so far as to put his hand on my shoulder. "Look here, I believe you. I really do. You're not the kind of guy to be brawling with a knife in his pocket. And I'm glad you've started talking. It's important for someone in your situation to begin talking and thinking to find a way out. Let's talk this through together. So let's suppose you're having an affair with the most beautiful girl in town. If you go out with a good-looking girl, you know there are hazards involved and you have to take precautions. You know the ropes. You know what can happen. People are watching, and some of them are jealous. There is no obvious danger at this stage. It's just a, how shall I put it, potential danger. You're threatened on two fronts. Firstly, there is the girl's father, who's a man of influence in town. Secondly, there's that rowdy you were fighting with in the tavern. I was told that he's after your girl and that he's jealous to the point of rage. He doesn't miss a thing, and could even tell you how many times a day she goes to the bathroom. And you, careless as you are, meet this girl at the apartment of an acquaintance, and you do that, not just once, but several days in a row. Inexcusable behaviour. Did it never occur to you that it might be a trap? You fell right into it because people were watching. That rowdy friend of yours has given evidence that you attacked him with a knife. You can deny it all you want. But even if we assume that he poses no danger, there is still the girl's father. You can't get away from him. He knows everything, and he's going to move heaven and earth to get back at you. And consider the influence he has in town."

My head was swimming. I'd lost all perception of time. I didn't know how many hours I'd spent in the cell under the wan light of that single bulb in the ceiling. My brain was blocked. As much as I tried, I still couldn't see any connection between my situation and the presence of Grey Eyes. He'd said that he wanted to talk to me about something serious, something that might interest me, and intimated that it might interest someone else. But who? "No sir," I said to myself, noticing the ominous glitter in his eyes, "you didn't come all the way here just to tell me you've been with Sonia. And not to insult her in front of me. You wouldn't spend your time on those kinds of trivial matters." Grey Eyes was of the same opinion. "Let's not waste time on superfluous details," he coaxed. Then, all of a sudden, he asked, "Aren't you even interested in knowing how Sonia is?" I was too weak to take a punch at him, not to mention the fact that I'd likely have missed and the punch would have come back to me like a boomerang. "She cleans stables," he informed me in his investigator tone, with the assurance of a man who was untouchable. "I must say, I felt sort of sorry for her when I saw her there with all the cows. And that slobbering idiot around her all the time. Can you imagine Sonia in miner's boots, dressed as a peasant, with her hair tucked under a woollen scarf and a spade in her hand, shovelling out the manure and filth? It suddenly occurred to me that day that you were the person who could save Sonia. It was cold out. The ground was frozen and there was Sonia, standing in the manure with that idiot after her all the time. Not a pleasant sight. Maybe this was the reason why I was taken by that base emotion called pity. Yes, I felt sorry for her, really, from the bottom of my heart, and left instructions that they keep the idiot off her. That at least will help. But Sonia is losing it, every hour she spends in that goddamned place, and sooner or later, she will have lost it all. So it occurred to me that a way might be found to save her. But that was a couple of months ago. I thought of you. It was just a vague idea and it's probably too early to talk about it. What I mean is, about the two of us. I was always convinced that you would help Sonia if you ever had a chance to do so. I am here to give you that chance and to get poor Sonia out of that godforsaken hell hole that will be the end of her sooner or later."

There was a certain quiver in his voice as he spoke those last words. Who'd have doubted that Grey Eyes was suffering, that his words were coming, as he claimed, from the bottom of his heart? I thought of my knife as I watched his Adam's apple rise and fall, and how it would make a swift job of him. If only I had it with me hidden in the right leg of my trousers. But I'd placed the knife in the care of my friend, the plump barmaid, and as a result, I had no choice but to swallow this filth, too, as I'd swallowed everything else he'd spewed at me since he'd come into my cell. I don't know how he interpreted my silence. If it's true that silence speaks a language of its own, he should have understood that I wanted nothing but to kill him. And I could have done it, could have put the knife to his throat and slain him like a ram. But either silence does not speak, or he didn't understand the language of my silence. Or he was interpreting it the way he wanted. "Sonia's life lies in your hands," he said, "and you must do everything you can to save her. I don't need an answer right away. For the moment, I will issue orders for your release. You can go home, have a bath, something to eat, and get a bit of sleep. When you've recovered, think about what I've said. It's about Sonia's very survival, and what happens to her is up to you. It's the first thing you must think about when you've recovered. The second thing will be the proposal I'm going to make to you. But you don't need to respond to that right away either. All I want to do right now is to remind you of something. You're not a stupid guy, and you understand full well the mess you're in. But let's let bygones be bygones. You were expelled from university, have no degree and will probably spend the rest of your life in this hole, surrounded by dust and cement. You once had an opportunity to start a new life. Did you ever think it might be possible to return to that life? That you could resume your studies where you left off? And above all, have you ever thought about the possibility of a new start with Sonia? Alright, you've probably dreamt about it, but you would never have thought of it as a reality. You probably said to yourself, 'They're only daydreams I'm having.' But I've come to tell you that there's a way to turn them into reality. The only condition is that you want to help Sonia. You'll see that you can escape from the misery in which most people around you are living like worms. You can get away from the dust, from the work at the factory. You can rid yourself of that lunatic Xhoda and that wolf pack here in town who you almost ran a knife through. You can be free… Listen to what I'm saying. You do not belong to the dregs of society. It would be a shame for someone like you to vegetate like the rest of them."

My interlocutor was enthused by his own honesty. I could see it in the way he talked and in the way he looked at me, and I almost believed everything he said. But I knew his kind and had an ominous sense of foreboding. I wasn't jealous of him because of Sonia, and I didn't believe he'd come at Sonia's request. I had this foreboding because, my

God, there was nothing I could have wanted more. All my
dreams could come true, I felt, if only I had the willpower.
I desperately wanted to start over again, to see Sonia once
more and sleep with her, to lie beside her body and find
peace. What more could I long for in my misery? He had
me in the grip of his grey eyes. But my brain was empty. I
was ready to fall to my knees and beg him to get me out of
there and take me to Sonia, come what may. I asked him
what he wanted. My voice wavered and sounded foreign to
me, like the voice of a ghost risen from the grave and
calling from another world. "Nothing," he replied. And I
thought to myself: "So that's what Lucifer looks like
coming for my soul. "Nothing in particular," he added,
leaning over towards me. "Just some good times between
the two of us, a few relaxed conversations about what's
going on. I don't mean about you, I mean about a few
people you might know, or might not know. We could form
a club or an association, whatever you want to call it, you,
Sonia and I. Not now, not today, but sometime when, at
your wish and with my intervention, we could succeed in
getting her out of that place and away from all the manure
and piss. You will feel strong, both as a human being and as
a man, and you will experience what strength can achieve.
You will see that only the weak, the idiots and the losers are
vegetating in the amorphous, filthy dregs of a society in
which all human virtues amount to nothing, where you are
nothing but a zero, to be beaten, insulted, humiliated and
oppressed. You are intelligent enough to understand. Not
much will be asked of you, as I said earlier. We'll just meet
from time to time, the two of us, in a park, a cafe, for a
walk, or for dinner. Wherever you want. You can choose the
venue. We'll talk about life, about people, what students are
thinking about nowadays, what motivates them, how they
spend their free time, who they complain about, who they
make fun of, what they're saying and doing nowadays, or
what they intend to do. I don't need an answer from you
yet. I am going out to have you released. Go back home

and have a good rest. And don't speak to anyone about what we've been discussing, ever." His eyes were glowing. "Think it over, and everything will be alright. Otherwise…"

He didn't finish that last sentence. "I'll wait for you the day after tomorrow at the coffee shop of the Writers' Union," he added. "It's quiet there, a nice place. I play chess in the large clubroom in the afternoon. They pay attention to hygiene and you can meet people – important figures, artistes, and sometimes even beautiful women. So, I'll be expecting you. The day after tomorrow at about 6 p.m. If you don't show up, I'll assume you've turned down my offer. I'm giving you an opportunity. Don't let it slip through your fingers. Otherwise…"

By the time I'd mustered myself to form a resolute 'no'! inside me, he was gone. The word 'otherwise' echoed in the cell, and the 'no' never passed my lips. It raged in my mind like a wild beast throwing itself at a cage, desperate to get out. But the bars wouldn't give way. The cry was trapped inside me, suffocated and perished. The walls heard nothing. The word 'otherwise' hovered above me in my cell like a menacing bird. The door opened and someone came in. It was the ruddy-faced officer with the huge paws. He stretched one of them towards me and pulled me up by the chin. The dim light bulb blinded me. His teeth were unusually white, strong and even. I'd never seen such white, strong and even teeth before. Then I then noticed he had a rag in his hand and had only pulled me up to wipe my face off. It wasn't a rag, but a pad of cotton wool drenched in alcohol. My face burned. Then he handed me a comb for my hair and ordered me to beat the dust out of my clothes. "No one touched you here, you understand?" he blurted. "You got all these cuts and bruises from fighting off some thug you don't know and never saw again. Now get out of here! And not a word from you. If we ever get our hands on you again, you'll be much the worse for wear."

He saw me out. "Good-bye," he said, probably from

force of habit. "Good riddance," I hissed to myself. The street was empty. The whole town seemed empty. In one corner of the sky a sallow sun sagged, half-hidden by dark clouds. But it was enough to blind me. Like the dim light bulb in my cell.

Big drops of rain splashed onto the pavement, spraying the dust in all directions. I looked up. "Why don't you just empty those clouds on us, damn sky?" I complained. "Are you afraid the refugees are going to get wet? They've arrived now, dirty sky. And you're as filthy as the underwear of a cheap whore." They were all gone. "I'm the only one left here, left to eat the meatballs which Arsen Mjalti has probably made from dog meat, and to drink the raki which he's pissed into to increase its strength. But better Arsen's urine than nitrate. Arsen's urine won't harm anyone, as opposed to the nitrate which sends you to an early grave, off to the other world. I don't mean the world where the refugees have now arrived. I mean the world of nothing, of eternal dreamless sleep. I've got to get some sleep myself, with dreams or without them."

Half drunk, I stumbled towards the entrance of the apartment building and sat down on the stairs. If I hadn't, I would have fallen over anyway. "Another world... Another world. I want to go to another world!" I shouted to my mother on her way home who discovered me at the bottom of the stairwell. She cursed. I'm not sure what she cursed – me, the other world, or the lack of lighting in the stairwell. Getting me into the apartment, slumped over her shoulder, was no small feat. In any case, we finally staggered up to the apartment door, which she opened. Father appeared in the doorway and everything went easier from then on. With father propping me up on one side, and mother on the other, I made it into the kitchen where they dumped me onto the sofa. I was so drunk that everything on the surface of the smooth floor below me seemed to be floating around and around in a maelstrom. It made me dizzy. With me on the ship were mother and father, sitting in their armchairs on the other side of the table. I was rolling over the waves, and so were their four faces, two of father's and two of mother's, all those sad faces staring at the son who had let them down. I wanted to ask them if they'd ever placed any hope in me to start with. My parents, my poor parents were now old. Even my drunken eyes could see that. I pulled myself off the sofa ship, navigating in their direction and smothered their faces in kisses. There were four pairs of lips, eight eyes, and eight arms like a Buddha statue. "I am Buddha!" I blurted out to the four faces. They had tears in their eyes, and I couldn't understand why they were crying. Maybe it was the great disappointment in their lives, the self-proclaimed Buddha who was now back in their kitchen as a result of a little accident – the pee of Dori's son. If the kid hadn't peed down the back of my neck, I'd now be huddled with a group of refugees in a camp somewhere. A refugee Buddha.

My parents helped me to my room, got me undressed and tucked me into bed, covering me with the quilt. I had a dreamless night and slept the sleep of the dead. When I woke up, Dori appeared in my reverberating skull. "Where are you, Dori?" I pleaded, as I looked at the light shining in through the window.

# 16

I'd had a dreamless night and slept like a log for I don't know how many hours. Thirteen or fourteen, maybe more, maybe less. It didn't matter. I wanted the clock to stand still, but it kept moving. Time was doing its inexorable job to the rhythm of eternity, not caring whether I'd had a dreamless night or slept like a log. Time continued its journey just the same as thirteen or fourteen hours earlier, maybe more, maybe less, while I was stealing through the streets, back from the police station, trying quite superfluously not to be seen. The town was deserted. I managed to reach the empty apartment because for some inexplicable reason my parents were out, which was a big relief to me. I had no wish to explain where I'd been, no reason to talk at all. The silence and the void were just what I craved. My bedroom was cold and empty, just what I needed. My bed and the old clothes closet were silent, frigid and ugly. I quivered at the thought of total abandonment, undressed, slid into bed, and pulled the covers up over me. They didn't seem to oppose my wish for the clock to stand still as I slept. But time hadn't stood still. It was light outside when I woke up. My first impression was that nothing had changed, but the world was still the same as it had been. My second impression was of acute pain in my face, my neck, my shins and my ribs. I was in terrible shape. The mirror offered me irrefutable proof of my swollen and battered face. It hid nothing, neither the blue swelling on my right cheek nor the cut in the left corner of my mouth. To add to this, there were scratches and a couple of other bruises here and there, but nothing too important. The mirror also showed me that I'd grown a beard, but that was normal and didn't bother me much. Beards grew overnight, too, when the body was sleeping, the step before death. With ruthless honesty, the mirror seemed to want to remind me that I belonged to the dead, either for a time or forever. I had a shower and then started to shave in front of the mirror. There was fear in my eyes. Time hadn't stood still. It was still running, mercilessly, following its own eternal rhythm, whether my beard grew or not. I'd soon have to give him an answer. Grey Eyes was waiting.

Although I shaved and used all the cosmetics I could find to blot out the massacre on my face, it still wouldn't go away. On the contrary, the signs of the beating were more evident than ever. They weren't exactly telltale love bites. My whole face was a battlefield. I decided to go out anyway. I didn't have the impression that a battered face would raise any eyebrows, even if it looked like the face of a dead man. Anyone who saw my battered face showed no sign of reaction, which made it obvious to me that the tale of my adventure with the police had been the talk of the town. For the few who were ever released, and I was to count myself lucky at being one of them, a battered face was the smallest of problems. It was all part of the game. A brief glance in the tavern between me and the barmaid was enough to confirm our silent understanding. There was no need to say a thing. She handed me a glass of cognac. "Don't worry," her eyes told me, "the object you gave me is in safekeeping." "Keep it," I thought, "in safekeeping or not, do whatever you want with it. I don't need a knife anymore." Yesterday was the final occasion for its purpose. If they hadn't detained me, I would have used it on Fagu. But they got me and Fagu survived. I had no more need of the knife. It was a primitive, vulgar weapon anyway. To do the deed properly, you have to stand face to face in front of your opponent and shove it into him at the right spot in the middle of the chest, just below the heart. Not to mention all the subsequent dangers involved. Even if you're really careful to find the right spot, it can sometimes go the other way around, that is, you get the opponent's knife in your stomach first and are dispatched to another world. And even if you're successful and manage to expedite your opponent, you're still faced with the prospect of imprisonment, a bullet or a noose. Whichever way you look at it, you lose. No, the classic dagger, the little knife you keep hidden somewhere, is not for me and never will be. It's dangerous, leaves traces and can cost you your neck.

I was disturbed to discover that I was talking to myself. The plump barmaid kept her eyes rivetted to me all the time as I talked and sipped at my cognac. She nodded in agreement as if she'd invaded my brain and could hear everything. For example, I mumbled to her and elaborated my thesis: "Suppose we fall out and become enemies, only as a hypothesis, as a mathematician would say. Let's suppose you fall out with me or I fall out with you. There could be an infinite number of causes for hostility between two people, mathematically speaking. As an example, I could be envious of the fact that you're doing so well in life, that you have a husband who treats you well – if I, assuming I were a woman, had a husband who constantly beat me up. Or I could be jealous of the fact that you have money and I don't, that you're attractive and I'm not, that you're in good health and I have rickets, that all the men are after you whereas none of them want me and run away from me as if I had the plague. In short, let's assume there's hostility between us for some insignificant reason. Or, if you prefer, for some good reason, something significant – some people live in the illusion of their own significance. Did it ever occur to you, my corpulent friend, that I could kill you? Of course not with the knife. I'm not crazy enough to stab you to death and get killed myself. What I mean is I could kill you and not suffer any consequences. In fact, if things went well, I could even get something out of it – satisfaction, prosperity, happiness, power."

I fled the tavern. If I'd stayed any longer under the constant observation of the barmaid, I would have screamed. I was supposed to be very upset and depressed, and I wasn't. I'd been offered a knife, but not the classic, run-of-the-mill dagger to be rammed into someone's body, slicing tissue and muscles, breaking bones, revealing the internal organs of the chest, piercing the heart, and spilling out the guts. No, I'd been offered an invisible knife that I could use to get rid of someone without having to shove a knife into him. My victim could be lying peacefully in bed with his wife, his fiancée or his lover, filling her with new life, and he would experience a sudden divine pain as I stabbed him without his even knowing it and pushed the knife deep into him. And the next day, I'd meet him in the tavern, have a glass or two of cognac with him and clasp his hand in mine, drenched in his blood.

The smoke of the chimneystack rose straight into the air in a black column. Even if I screamed, playing the role of the barking dog, it'd still have risen vertically. (Let the dogs bark.) I could now hear real barking from the gypsy quarter, but didn't bother to look around to see if there might be a caravan passing. The caravans probably didn't even know there was a gypsy quarter down by the river. They went their way, the devil knows where, paying no attention to the barking of the gypsy dogs, just as they'd have paid no attention to me if I tried to imitate a dog and bark at them. The assistant with the bonnet and the dreary, puffy face paid no particular attention to me as I went into the laboratory and asked, in a loud voice, if anyone was there. I managed to find out that Dori was once again at a meeting and that Lulu was still in the hospital. Vilma hadn't yet returned to work. Puff-face claimed not to know why. "Indolent sloth," I thought to myself, "you know very well why Vilma is absent." I casually raised my hand to cover the bruises on my face. The sloth stared at me. "It's nothing important," I modestly denied to satisfy her curiosity. "I was invited out to dinner last night and was treated royally, as you can see." She laughed. The laugh came so unexpectedly that it put me in good form. "They certainly served you well," she replied, adding, "To hell with all of them. Watch out, boy, and take good care of yourself. If you're on their list, you won't be around for long." Then the sloth turned her back to me and shuffled over to her corner of the lab where only her white bonnet could be seen under a dusting of cement. "Thanks," I whispered, more to myself than anyone else because she was too far away to hear me. She wouldn't have heard me even if she'd been standing beside me because I was mumbling. I wanted to give myself a bit of courage. Then I went out.

After I left the laboratory, I stood for a minute on the square in front of the plant, and stared at the column of black smoke rising into the sky. My ears were ringing with the barking of dogs, of that pack of mongrels, starving, freezing, kicked around, and ending up with a hunk of poisoned liver. "What about me?" I thought. "When am I going to get my piece of liver?" I can remember the exact moment this thought flashed through my body like a jolt of lightning. Everything that happened afterwards blurs into a haze. It was as if something hard had struck me over the head, like a crowbar or a crank handle. But no one struck me, either with a crowbar or a crank handle or anything else. So it wasn't a form of amnesia. Up to that day, that is to say, up to the day I woke up with a scarred face and went out to the plant to find Dori, the tape of my memory had recorded all events in a more or less regular way. But after that, there was nothing on the tape. It wasn't that I'd lost my capacity to record. The tape was blank because there was nothing more to put on it, with the exception of a couple of minor incidents which served as a conclusion to this chapter of my existence.

# 17

The tape of my memory ends in noise. The noises I hear in the form of screams, barking dogs, or cries from the dead. My ears have been ringing day and night. Insects are buzzing around in my skull, trying to burst it. But my skull, like everyone else's, is strong. It's constructed according to the laws of nature to protect and preserve that high-tech centre of physical existence – the brain. One of the chambers of the brain stores the tape of memory. But my chamber's been immersed in fifteen, sixteen, seventeen or more years of sediment, a thick and gooey layer of mud, the bestial monotony of my life since that time. Yet here and there in the depths of the chamber, noises – screams, barking dogs, cries from the dead – still crack open, break their way through the sediment and rise to the surface like bubbles. They're the last events of that part of my life, recorded on the tape of my memory, the final days before I entered a new phase where I'd come to vegetate in the sediment of urban monotony, with death already inside me.

I'm no longer sure of the exact sequence of events. I can't say what happened first and what happened later. In fact, I don't know whether there was any connection between the events or whether it was all a blind coincidence. But there's one thing I can say for sure. I had no power to stop them. I might have been able to stop some meaningless act of my own, but it wouldn't have had any connection to subsequent events.

On the prescribed day and at the prescribed hour, I approached the building of the Writers' Union, where A.P., the grey-eyed investigator and son of the minister was waiting for me. I ascribe no particular significance to the fact that I went. My appearance at the Writer's Union would have had meaning if I'd been carrying a knife with me, because I'd have agreed to meet him with the sole purpose of slaughtering him. But I went without a knife. When I got to the iron door of the Writers' Union, I didn't make any attempt to look inside to see if Grey Eyes was there.

I turned around and took off, without ever finding out. And yet, I made the discovery of my life. I found out once and for all that I was simply not capable of using a knife. I was incapable of killing myself, and was equally incapable of blotting out anyone else's existence. I realised this the moment I retreated from the iron door of the Writers' Union. Grey Eyes was probably waiting behind it to make a deal with me. I felt ashamed. I knew that from then on, I'd be squirming between life and death, writhing in my last throes, not dead and not alive. I'd stumbled into an anonymity denuded of hope. Behind me stretched a past, dripping with venom. And in front of me lay a future that I was completely indifferent to. As I walked away from the iron door of the Writers' Union, I knew that the most convincing argument for me to continue living was my inability to escape life. My inadequacy. But maybe it was my destiny to live a banal, mediocre existence in the mud and filth of a little town, condemned to while away the coming years amidst the suffering and tragedies of others. Death is eternal sleep. Living death is eternal torture.

Dori was the first to be arrested. At least, that's the way I remember it. I don't recall if I'd already lost my job in the lab when Dori was taken into custody or if the man in the metal cage summoned me to his office after Dori's arrest, to tell me that I was fired. It's not important anyway, so I'll say that Dori's arrest happened first. It was winter and the tavern was packed to the rafters. I'd seen Dori several times in the past few days hanging out with a couple of engineers. His relationship with his fiancée was not going well and he drowned his sorrows in alcohol. Dori was arrested as he was leaving a meeting of the technical committee.

They handcuffed him in front of everyone, and recited the usual, tiresome formula: 'In the name of the people, you are under arrest.' That's what I heard. I didn't see anything myself. I saw nothing of Dori or his bewildered smile which always had a touch of irony to it. I had to recall the smack in the face I'd got from him one day when I was so drunk that I started blabbing loudly about something unhygienic. He'd slugged me because he didn't want to end up in prison with me. Cautious old Dori had now landed in a cell himself, as if to confirm the warning given to me by the sleepy lab assistant when she told me to watch out. 'If you're on their list, you won't be around for long'. Dori had apparently been on their list. I never discovered why, and never heard when they convicted him behind closed doors. No one even informed me ten years later when he got out of prison. He was in appalling shape. After that, we'd go out bingeing together whenever we had the money. He'd never talk about the past.

Then there was the day I was summoned to see the man in the metal cage. He coughed, scratched himself, smacked his lips, and looked me over from head to toe. He explained to me that, in accordance with the labour code, I was fired because I hadn't appeared on the job for three days in a row without good cause. He was probably right in his reasoning. I don't remember how many days I'd been absent from the lab. I would leave home in the morning. My first stop would be the tavern, where I always got waylaid. This of course, had nothing to do with the infamous deficiencies in the public transportation system. I drank and drank and drank. I never got enough. From morning to night. So I had no reason to contradict the man in the metal cage. I'd probably not been absent just for three days, enough for the stipulations of the labour code, but for far more than that. I said nothing and went out with a feeling of total abandonment, not knowing quite where I was headed. On my tracks right behind me was the man-eating tiger, poised to attack and gobble me up. I kept walking, waiting for the wonder of nature to occur, to feel the claws dig into my back, to suffer the teeth biting into my shoulders and to experience the end of my existence. But somehow, my end didn't come. My end was out there somewhere, but it didn't come. The tiger was stalking me, taking note of my agony, and had me right in front of its cave-like jaws. Like a blindman at the edge of a cliff, I'd advance on my own two feet and hurl myself into the depths. I had a concrete vision of my end, either being ripped to pieces by the tiger or torn to shreds on the rocky crags in the chasm of my life, squashed by the wheel of fate. And I didn't know that I had already reached my end, long ago. Could fate have had any more horrible end in store for me?

At the time, I saw no real connection between my fall and the fact that I hadn't gone to meet Grey Eyes. Three or four or five days of bingeing and drunken stupor following Dori's arrest were enough to put me out of keel forever. It never occurred to me to blame Grey Eyes or Xhoda. Nor the guy in the metal cage. But they were the real people behind my fall. Grey Eyes had taken Sonia away from me, and Xhoda had spirited Vilma off and hid her from me. The man in the metal cage had stolen everything else, in exchange for my employment record booklet, which he handed back to me. As I didn't know what to do with it, I hurled it through the iron bars of the cage where it landed on the floor.

A few days later, a special courier of the military recruitment office in town knocked on our apartment door. I was at home, half drunk, half demented. The courier handed me an official letter, stamped and sealed. I had to sign for it. The Fatherland was calling. The Fatherland needed me. It happened just a few days after I'd sneaked out of the office of the man in the metal cage.

# 18

There's only a little bit left. Then the tape of my memory will have reached its conclusion. Everything after that lies in a void, just like when you wander aimlessly in a dark tunnel, with bats flying around your face and body. A pitch-black tunnel. You don't know how you got into it and you don't know if you'll ever get out again. The noise on this last part of the tape is muffled, a vague whisper, dogs barking in the background, a choir sending a blind caravan off into the tunnel, polyphonic cries from the dead – and Vilma's voice is there with them. A wail of agony, the shriek of an innocent child.

It was summer and I'd been wrested away from the world. The Fatherland needed me and I answered the call. In lieu of a rifle, I received a shovel. The shovel was soon replaced by a pickaxe, and the pickaxe by a spade and then by other tools. The Fatherland didn't seem to be in need of me as a rifleman, and it didn't even need my blood. I spent my days rotting away on a farm, a so-called military agricultural enterprise, raising chickens, sheep and pigs. I did the raising, but I felt like I was putrefying inside. Maybe this, my internal decay, was the reason the Fatherland didn't want my blood. I must admit I had nothing left to defend in the Fatherland, no stone, no grain of sand, no father, no mother. They all belonged to someone else – for example, to the commissar of the enterprise, who not only had a thick neck and a bloated face, but who carried a revolver in the back of his trousers. Its handle stuck out from under his jacket. For him, we unarmed soldiers were all hornless devils, worse than the optimistic devils of the limestone-crushing unit at the plant. For us, he wasn't a mini-Zeus, but the Almighty himself, who reminded us every day from the moment we opened our eyes to the time we fell asleep at night that we were to worship only him, six times a day, before and after every meal, and that we were to bow to him, keep quiet and pay attention all the time. That's enough to describe him. Otherwise, he wasn't particularly interesting.

The telegram arrived in the afternoon. It was a hot day, and there was an unbearable stench in the cowsheds. I was lying in the shade of a poplar tree, and my brain was just as empty as the cows', when someone called me over from the huts. The call, and then curses, rang out several times before it ever occurred to me that a telegram had arrived for me. My weary brain was hardly able to process information. Someone had taken the time to send me a telegram here at the end of the earth to inform me that the planet was still revolving. I signed for it and got the curious piece of paper with some pale letters typed on it. Pressed into the paper was Vilma's cry of despair which exploded into my face when I unfolded it. "Vilma dead. Funeral tomorrow. 2 p.m. Lulu." I stuffed the telegram into my pocket and went back to lie under the poplar tree. Vilma was dead. The funeral would be tomorrow at two in the afternoon. That's what Lulu'd written and she wasn't a person to lie. I hid my face in the palms of my hands which were now moist with tears. My brain went numb and I could understand only the message that Vilma was dead. It was so numb that it wasn't in a position to analyse or ask the big question: "How did she die? What happened?" All I could think of was that her divine being was now in another world, she'd soared off to where she belonged, in paradise. Our hell on earth with all the devils in town was not for her, and could not keep her. "Vilma is dead," I murmured with my face in my hands. My palms were overflowing with tears.

It seemed superfluous to ask my superiors for permission to attend the funeral. Not only were they unworthy to share the intimacy of Vilma's death with me, they would also start asking me about my relations with Vilma and I wouldn't have been able to provide a satisfactory answer to get the authorization I needed. I left the farm without saying a word, slinking down a path and disappearing into a ditch which had once contained a stream. I eventually reached the road which connected the villages of the area to the provincial town. It was a dusty track full of potholes and rarely used by cars. The sun hovered like a red-hot iron disk above my head. All the time I wondered what questions my superiors would have asked if I'd been stupid enough to request authorization – which they'd never have given me. "Who is this woman anyway?" they'd have demanded. "Your mother, your sister, an aunt of yours, or your grand-mother?" And I wouldn't have known what to say. I wasn't sure what Vilma had meant to me. I'd never purposely wanted to get to know her, and I also never had enough time to be able to truly know her. Continuing down the road, with the red-hot disk suspended above my head, I was seized by anguish and a revelation. "Oh God," I murmured, "you bestowed a blessing on me and I didn't even see it." A shiver ran down my spine. "God," I cried out loud, "was she my dead blessing? Is this what you're now revealing to me?" My cry faded into the silent wasteland around me, and I continued on my way, convincing myself that the disk above me was the origin of my morbid thoughts.

I went on foot to start with, then hitched a lift, hopped aboard a train, and was always on the lookout for patrols. I finally got into town late that night. The lights were out. The whole centre was plunged into darkness. Maybe there was a power shortage. Sparks rose from the cement works chimneystack and were silently snuffed out by the night sky. But there was one light, in Xhoda's house. It was a pale, shimmering glimmers. I leaned against the pine tree. My legs had led me there of their own accord, to the pine tree of my childhood, just outside the wrought-iron fence. I could hear a muffled mourning, could sense a quivering of humanity, like wavering flames. Suddenly the lights went on. A natural reflex made me cower behind the tree, but there was no sense in my hiding. In the desolation, I was no more than an elusive shadow. I caught sight of Lulu with a group of people near the entrance. They came down the staircase quietly, paced through the courtyard and stopped at the fence. I ducked, and my forehead was covered in sweat. Then Lulu left the group and disappeared down a turn of the road with someone I didn't know. I had no more reason to stand around. I was dizzy. The other person walked Lulu home and said good-bye to her. I hid behind a corner of the apartment building until she was gone. Lulu was now in her apartment. There was no reaction when I rang the doorbell. I let it ring for quite a while until I heard a shuffle of steps and a faint, frightened voice inquiring: "Who's there?" I told her who I was and the door opened. Lulu broke into tears and threw her arms around me. I closed the door behind us and looked into Lulu's distorted face. "She poisoned herself," Lulu stammered with swollen eyes. "I didn't know. I couldn't have saved her. How could I have known anyway?"

Lulu trembled. She looked like death personified. I took her head between my hands and pressed it to my chest, stroking her hair. "What happened?" I asked, with my mouth close to her ear. She stepped back. Her body, her whole being was shaking. Without saying a word, she went to put the coffeepot on the stove and made coffee, not even asking if I wanted any. It was the same reflex she had every time I visited her. I sat down on the sofa beside the kitchen table. She sank onto the chair across from me and waited in silence for me to finish my cup. When I'd drunk my coffee, she slowly stood up. "Vilma," she said icily, "poisoned herself this morning. She swallowed some pesticide with a terrible name I can't remember. I recall that her father used it to spray the vineyards. She locked herself in her room. When her family heard the groaning, they had to knock the door down to get in, but it was too late. She died in hospital."

I turned as white as a sheet right then. I wanted to throw up, yet there was nothing for me to vomit but the coffee I'd just drunk. She must have gone through the same agony as Max, I thought. I almost said so to Lulu. She didn't know the story about Max so I thought it might be better not to mention it. But maybe she did know after all. She knew everything else about Vilma. Maybe this was why she was staring at me as if I were a common criminal. I wanted to tell her that I wasn't a criminal and that I'd had nothing to do with Max's death, at least not directly. Max had been poisoned by a gypsy called Sherif who'd taken a piece of lamb liver drenched in a poison used to kill wild dogs – not that Max was wild. I'd nothing against Vilma herself. I'd only wanted to get back at her father, the guard dog of my childhood. I'd never had anything against Vilma. Never.

A terrible suspicion rose in my throat and caused me to gasp for breath. As Lulu stared at me in provocative silence, my numb brain finally managed to ask the question: "Why did she poison herself? She had nothing on her conscience. She never committed a sin in her life. So, why would she do it? Why?" I turned to see Lulu at the window, staring into the dark. "Lulu," I stuttered, "tell me what happened. She had no reason… Why would she do it? I've been travelling all day and I'm exhausted. Lulu, you're the first person I've talked to."

Lulu pressed the palms of her hands to her temples. Her face was pale. She started to sob and couldn't speak for a while. "She was raped," she finally replied. For me it was like a scream from the depths, a scream as piercing as a pointed spear, and the spear was now embedded deep in my breast. I couldn't breathe. "She was raped," repeated Lulu, as if to plant the spear even deeper. "Four days ago, at home, in the room where she committed suicide. The guy waited around until everyone else had left. There was a wedding. Vilma didn't want to attend. Some cousin of hers from a village was getting married and everyone was going, except Vilma. I don't know why she didn't go, but it was her downfall. She was raped on a Sunday. Vilma was so gentle, and there wasn't anyone here to help her, either at the time of the rape, or when she took the poison. She was like an innocent lamb in the clutches of a wolf. And the wolf was called Fagu. He's the one who raped her."

I jumped to my feet and wanted to scream. If I hadn't bashed my head against the wall, I would have screamed so loudly as to wake up the whole building, the whole neighbourhood. The blood welled in my veins and my eyes were dimmed. The scream inside me was silenced. "You can break your skull if you want to, but it won't change anything," said Lulu, as if she were egging me on. "She's not coming back. She's dead. So go ahead and smash your head against the wall. I don't even know why I sent you the telegram. You never did anything for her, never had eyes to see or a heart to feel what was going on. Go ahead and bash your head against the wall a thousand times for all I care. What's done is done. Don't you think a girl is saying something to you when she invites you over? You didn't understand a thing, and behaved like an absolute fool, like those louts in the tavern who spend all their time with whores. Do you think you treated her any better than a whore? And she was ready to go to the ends of the earth with you. Go ahead and smash yourself into a pulp, but it won't bring Vilma back."

Lulu started to sob again. I had no choice but to let her vent all the rage pent up inside her. I wouldn't have been surprised if she'd lunged at me and gouged my eyes out. She wept and wept. Then she came over to me. "Don't listen to what I'm saying. It's not your fault. Even if you had behaved differently to Vilma, it would never have worked out. It wasn't your fault or hers. And even if you had got together, Xhoda would never have allowed it. Vilma knew that. So did the wolf, Fagu. I'm the only one who knows how she suffered from him, until he finally did her in. He never left her a moment's peace. He was always snooping, always one step behind her, day and night. The beast was ready to kiss the ground she walked on, to commit any crime imaginable for her. His rats were spying on us the day you came over to visit Vilma, and they were the ones who beat me up. You have no idea what we went through when they put you on the other shift and then sent you to the army. He was so crazed in his desire that he even went to Vilma's father and asked permission to marry her. Xhoda treated him like dirt. He told him he could only have his daughter if he could see the tips of his ears without a mirror, and added that even if he had forty daughters, he wouldn't give a single one of them to Fagu. Xhoda didn't know that Fagu couldn't be put off that easily. Now Xhoda's gone mad, tearing his hair out and crying in a loud voice. When he realised what had happened, he grabbed his pistol and ran though town to look for Fagu – to the tavern, the plant, and to his house. If he'd caught him, he would have killed him on the spot. But the police were faster. They arrested Fagu two days ago in Tirana. I don't know where they're holding him. They got two other guys today, too, the ones who had held watch for him, but I don't know who they are."

Lulu fell silent. Either she had no more to say or it was the first time that she'd noticed my bruised face. She froze for a second. "You don't have to bash your head against the wall," she whispered. "You'll only break your skull, not the wall." Lulu went into the next room and came back carrying a little bottle of spirits and a wad of cottonwool. "If you want to know what I think," she said firmly, "it would be best if you spent the night here on the couch. With the state you're in, you're going to frighten your family to death." She was right, not only about my face, but about my head and the wall. 'There's no sense in beating your head against the wall.' That's what everyone said. And those who tried it were sooner or later convinced by the hard logic of the wall. Those who weren't convinced, were soon left with a fractured skull. "You're right," I replied. "There's no sense in it. But, Lulu, how long are we going to go on getting our heads bashed in?" "Until you learn that you can't break your way through the wall," she said. I couldn't stay there any longer. If I had, I'd have smashed my head into a bloody pulp.

My parents couldn't have been more surprised if a Martian had appeared at their door. They weren't expecting me and, on top of this, I woke them up in the middle of the night. When you're jolted from your sleep, anything bad seems a hundred times worse than it really is. "Don't be afraid," I stammered. "I'm not coming from the police." My parents, who had gone through many trials and tribulations, asked no questions. They were just happy to see me alive. The bruises on my head and the bloodied tracksuit I was wearing were of no importance to them. They sensed right away why I'd turned up so suddenly, and they wanted to inform me in a lot of detail about the burial which was going to take place the next day. I stopped them in their tracks. My nerves could take no more of it and I had difficulty keeping my self-control. Father went back to bed. Mother asked if I was hungry. I told her that I didn't need any food but just wanted to wash. Mother set a kettle of water on the petroleum stove. I begged her to go back to bed, which she eventually did. But before she left the room, she came closer and looked at me searchingly. She took my head in her hands and pressed it to her breast. I yielded to her without understanding her motive. It was a gesture long forgotten, a gesture from the time of my childhood. "I washed your trousers a few days ago," she said, "the ones with the zips. There was an envelope in one of the back pockets, so I put it on the night table in your bedroom."

She went out, leaving me standing in the hall. The enigma of the envelope stayed with me. If there was an envelope, there must be a letter inside it. I couldn't remember having been given a letter or having stuck an envelope into my back pocket. Yet there was in fact an envelope on my night table. It was open. Mother had obviously read it. Father probably, too. He wouldn't have ignored an open envelope and a letter which mother had already read:

*You don't understand, and you never will. I'm sorry I offended you yesterday. I didn't want to. I didn't know you would be so hurt. I have an ominous feeling that we will not see one another anymore. Yet it can't be true because we will be seeing one another in the lab. You will be in your corner, I in mine, and between us will be Lulu. Oh God, what a senseless life we lead. I'm so sorry. V.*

I stood there with the letter in my hand. I had no idea whatsoever how I'd come to receive it. From the letter V, it was obvious who'd sent it. The words of the letter stuck into me like nails as I took my bath. I had an irresistible urge for something to drink. Tiptoeing into the kitchen, I opened a cupboard and found an open bottle of cognac hidden among several containers of cooking oil. I took it and got myself a glass. I sneaked back to my bedroom, knowing that I'd go crazy that night if I didn't have a bottle with me. I drank the first glass in one quick swill. The second one, too. The alcohol penetrated my bloodstream, taking possession of my sub-cortex. When I felt a bit better, I opened the letter and read it again. What offence was Vilma talking about? When had she ever hurt me? I downed two more glasses of cognac. And what didn't I understand, what would I never understand? "You beast," I said to myself, and had two more glasses until my brain slowly started to click in. Vilma probably meant that an immature being like me would never accomplish anything. And I wouldn't ever, either in life or in love, because I didn't know how to live. I didn't even know how to die.

I wondered how the enigmatic letter had ever reached me. My eyes focussed on the words "I have an ominous feeling". Her premonition was right. We never did see one another again. How long has it been now? The question weighed on me like a heavy stone around my neck. If I didn't find an answer, the stone would drag me down and drown me in a lagoon of depression. It was only when the bottle was empty that I felt the blockage in my brain release. Something glimmered like a thin ray of light penetrating a dark chamber. "Eureka!" I cried suddenly, filled with sudden joy. I was so happy that my eyes welled with tears. The rope with the stone weighing heavily around my neck was snapped and I could breathe freely again. The letter had been given to me by a little boy while I was drinking in the tavern. It was Hermes, messenger of the gods. I hadn't seen Vilma from that time on, and had forgotten the letter, just as I'd forgotten everything else. But what importance could it have? It all belonged to the past, to oblivion. Just as I did.

Vilma's funeral took place the next afternoon at two o'clock, just as Lulu had announced. I didn't leave the house all day. Although she couldn't fail to notice that I'd emptied a whole bottle of cognac and was still drunk when she woke me up in the morning as I lay sprawled over the quilt, mother said nothing and went to the store to buy me another bottle, making me promise not to go out. I gave her my word, not just to get the bottle of cognac, but also because, after a night of drunken stupor, I knew I wasn't in a position to control my actions. I willingly gave in to her pleading and was moved to tears. After the first couple of glasses I was swimming once more in the turbulent waters of my drunken state. The first vision I had was of my final meeting with Vilma in Lulu's apartment. And of my longing to plunge into the cascade of her flowing hair. Or was it into her eyes? I seized her by the shoulders and shook her back and forth between my wish to slap her in the face and my desire to kiss her. But between us stood Sonia, and I wasn't able to get past Sonia to reach Vilma. Vilma screamed. I saw her scream. She lay on her bed, her dressing gown shredded, her lips bleeding from Fagu's teeth and the blood of her virginity trickling between her thighs. It was a hot summer's day when the wolf attacked the lamb in her fold.

Mother wasn't upset that I'd broken my promise. At least, she didn't indicate any displeasure. I observed the funeral from a distance, and took care not to do anything stupid or to create an incident. Xhoda led the procession of mourners, followed by a group of young men bearing the coffin containing Vilma's body which they carried solemnly from Xhoda's house to the graveyard. Most of them were members of Fagu's gang. Fagu could count himself lucky that he'd been arrested by the police. Otherwise the gang would have torn him to pieces. I watched from a safe position. When it was all over, the men lowered the roped coffin into the grave and the gravediggers started dragging a cement slab towards the tomb to cover it. Xhoda tore his hair and screamed. To everyone's horror, he rushed forward and hurled himself into the grave. It was only with a lot of difficulty that they managed to haul him out.

"Don't try to find out where I am," said Dori. "I am in another world. We have also entered the other world."

A chill ran down my spine. I heard a creak and mother's head appeared in the doorway. "Come on in," I said. "If you have any more raki, bring it, will you?" I added. She honoured my request and brought me not only the raki, but a cup of coffee. Then she asked me if I wanted anything else. Mother stood in the doorway staring at me the whole time. I asked her to sit down, so she did, with her hands folded in her lap. "There's no one left in town," she whispered. "They've all gone." I guzzled my coffee in the hope that it'd soothe the terrible headache I'd got from the raki. She thought I hadn't heard her and repeated what she'd said. "They're all gone, the boys and girls, the men, even the little children."

I looked up. Mother was still gazing at me. Her eyes told me: "I know you wanted to get away, too, but it's good that you didn't leave. I'm so glad." I couldn't stand her glance a second longer. "What do you mean?" I demanded. "Who is gone? I don't know what you're talking about." "Yes you do, you know very well what I mean," she replied. "They are all gone." I thought about the ship that had carried them all across the sea, Dori with his second wife and children, Fagu after fourteen years in prison, and almost all the members of his gang. Sonia was probably gone, too. She would have left with her son who's now grown up. I was the only one left. I wondered why.

I went out. A lead-grey sky hung over the sleepy town. There was no one on the road out to the graveyard. I felt lonely and forsaken, but I was sure that there were others who'd stayed behind, either because they couldn't get away or because they didn't want to. I couldn't leave her lying in her cold grave, abandoned and forgotten. I couldn't forsake Ladi or Vilma either. How could I take off and just leave them there? This is the way it was supposed to be. It had nothing to do with the fact that Dori's little boy had peed down the back of my neck. That wasn't the reason I'd abandoned the refugee ship at the last minute. I'd have disembarked anyway.

The graves were covered in hoarfrost. I wasn't sure where Vilma's grave was, so it took me a while to find it. There she was, staring at me from the marble gravestone, a photo which made her look almost alive, her hair cascading over her shoulders. "I've come back," I whispered, and bent over her grave. "I finally made it." The ground was cold. My frozen fingers tried to scoop together a bit of earth. In Vilma's eyes I saw Ladi's, just I'd once seen Vilma in Ladi's eyes. "They are gone," I murmured to myself, "and I am still here. I will always be with you."

Just then I heard some steps and had the impression that someone was standing over me. I caught sight of the end of an iron bar hanging beside me and knew who it was. I didn't move, but stayed crouched over the grave. "Go ahead and do it, you lunatic, send me to the other world. Not where the refugees are. That's another world too, but I didn't want to go to that one. You've got the power to send me to the other world where your daughter is. Go ahead and do it, lunatic, go ahead..."

The iron bar dangled beside my head. I looked up. Xhoda the Lunatic's bloodshot eyes were staring at me. He turned away and slowly paced towards the gate of the cemetery. I don't know if it was tears that I saw in his eyes or whether it was the morning dew. "You lunatic!" I wanted to cry out. "You had it in your power to send me to the other world. But we were destined to be chained together for the rest of our days, to be the curse of one another, until none of us exist anymore, neither you the lunatic, nor me the loser, nor Grey Eyes the incarnation of evil."

# A Note by the Translators

Fatos Kongoli (b. 1944) is one of the most forceful and convincing representatives of contemporary Albanian literature. He was born in the central Albanian town of Elbasan and raised in the capital, Tirana. As a young adult, during the tense years of the Sino-Albanian alliance, he was sent to Red China to study mathematics. Kongoli chose not to publish any major literary works during the oppressive dictatorship in his country. Instead, he devoted his creative energies to a relatively obscure and apolitical career as a mathematician, and waited for the storm to pass. There was, as he subsequently noted in an interview, "no Marxist strategy for mathematics". His narrative talent and individual style only really emerged, at any rate, in the nineties, after the fall of the communist regime.

*The Loser* (Alb. *I humburi*) takes the reader initially back to a real event in March 1991 when, after almost half a century of Stalinist rule, thousands of impoverished Albanians clambered onto a rust-infested freighter which was anchored in the port of Durrës and forced the crew to sail the vessel across the Adriatic Sea to Italy. The scenes broadcast on television of the arrival of the ship, teeming with refugees, were apocalyptic. It seemed that everyone wanted to leave Albania and start a new life elsewhere. The vast majority of Albanian refugees, after fifty years of total isolation, had no idea what awaited them in the outside world, the fabled and marvellous West. It is to these events in Albania's troubled history and, in particular, to the frightening decades in communist Albania which preceded them that Fatos Kongoli alludes in this novel.

Yet *The Loser* is not a novel of emigration. At the last moment before his ship sets sail, the book's protagonist, Thesar Lumi, the 'loser' for whom all hope is futile, aban-

179

dons his companions, disembarks and walks home. The novel returns at this point to the long and numbing years of the Enver Hoxha dictatorship and revives the climate of terror and universal despair that characterized day-to-day life in Albania in the sixties and seventies. Lumi, whose fate in Albania's hermetic society has been sealed once and for all by a daringly clandestine love affair, returns to live a life of futility in a universe with no heroes. Far from the active protagonist struggling to control his destiny or even from the staid but positive hero of socialist realism, Lumi is incapable of action and incapable of living. He is the voice of all the 'losers' who glimpse the silver clouds on the horizon and know full well that they will never reach them. "It was my destiny to live a banal, mediocre existence in the mud and filth of a little town, condemned to while away the coming years amidst the suffering and tragedies of others."

When it was first published in 1992, in what for Albania was a comparatively large edition, *The Loser* found immediate success among the reading public. There were few Albanians who could not identify with the confessional monologue, the secret and doomed loves, and the relentless psychological torment of Thesar Lumi. *The Loser* has been described as the most important Albanian novel to emerge from the post-communist era.

# A Note on the Translators

**Robert Elsie** (b. 1950, Vancouver, Canada) is a leading specialist in Albanian affairs. He is the author of over forty books, primarily on Albania and its culture, including literary translations from Albanian, and of many articles and research papers. He currently lives in The Hague, in the Netherlands. See www.elsie.de and www.albanianliterature.net.

**Janice Mathie-Heck** (b. 1950, Jasper, Canada) is a teacher, poet, translator, editor and literary critic, who lives in Calgary, Alberta. Her articles and poems have appeared in *The Gauntlet, Freefall, Le Chinook, Filling Station, Jeta e re* and *Illyria*. She has collaborated with Robert Elsie in translating and editing Albanian literature.